THE STORY OF
GUNNAR
HANSEN

JOHN C. DAILEY

Also By John C. Dailey

Front cover image: "Canoe on Lake Shore" by John L. Peyton
Back cover image: "Solo Portage" by John L. Peyton
Page x "Map E-15" W. A. Fisher Co.
Page 2, picture of "Emma" public domain

Cover design by Caroline K. Green

Printed in the United States of America

ISBN: 978-0-9986044-8-0

Gunnar Charles Hansen is a life-long resident of Minnesota except for the eleven years he served in the Marine Corps. As a young man, he spent part or all of his summers guiding canoe trips in the Quetico Provincial Park and the Boundary Waters Canoe Area Wilderness, or BWCAW. Now, at age seventy-three, he's setting out on a canoe trip in the Quetico Park, hoping to reconnect spiritually with his wife, Kathleen, who died in 2008.

For those of you who are not familiar with the type of canoe trip described in the story, a brief explanation might be helpful. In essence, we're talking about loading your food, clothes, cooking gear, tent, sleeping bag, and other necessities into pack sacks. Once assembled, the packs are placed in a canoe along with your fishing gear, life jackets and paddles, and you're on your way. One of the most popular areas for taking such a trip in North America is Quetico Provincial Park in Ontario and the adjoining Boundary Waters Canoe Area Wilderness in Minnesota.

But don't be misled. The canoe trip is just the fabric around which the rest of the tale is constructed, the great and undying love Gunnar has for his wife of thirty years, Kathleen. Gunnar exemplifies courage and faith in spite of adversity, and honor and love for God and country. While this is a book of fiction, there are references to real persons, places, things and events.

Quetico Provincial Park and the lakes Gunnar visits are real. His canoe trip takes place in 2018, two years before the park was closed due to the COVID-19 pandemic. In 2021, forest fires enveloped portions of the central and western parts of the park, which affected at least 14% of the park and made it difficult to portage and camp in the burned areas. High water levels in 2022 caused flooding in the western part of the park, affecting many lakes and campsites.

Because of the aforementioned natural disasters, the canoe trip route that Gunnar followed may no longer be possible. It may be years before things return to the way they were.

For those interested in following along in more detail the route of Gunnar's canoe trip as described in the book, please refer to Map E-15 from the W.A. Fisher Co. in Virginia, Minnesota. A map detailing his journey also can be found in the pages of this book.

John C. Dailey
March, 2024

ACKNOWLEDGEMENTS

This book could not have happened without the encouragement and help of my wife, Patricia.

The following consultants generously provided candid advice and information to help ensure the accuracy of my writing. Any mistakes in the novel are mine and mine alone:

- J. David Bone, platoon commander, 1st Recon Battalion, captain, USMC, Vietnam, 1966. Retired judge of the 7th Judicial Circuit, State of Illinois.

- Daniel Hallam, MD, PhD. General Surgeon, Springfield Clinic, Springfield, IL.

- Forrest G. Keaton, JD. Retired U.S. Air Force, Judge Advocate Division, Jacksonville, IL.

- David Lieber, MD. Urologist, Blessing Health System, Quincy, IL.

- Stuart Osthoff, publisher of *The Boundary Waters Journal*. Professional canoeing and fishing guide, Ely, MN.

- William V. Taylor, Jr., sergeant, USMC. Former member, Charlie Company, First Battalion, Third Marines, Vietnam, 1967-68. Author of *On Full Automatic.*

- James W. Veenstra, MD, Retired pathologist, former Army National Guard.

Thanks also to Kris and Doug Cameron of Hawk Ridge Art in Duluth, Minnesota, who gave me permission to reproduce paintings from my collection of John L. Peyton's artworks for the front and back covers of this book.

I also wish to thank W.A. Fisher Map Co. of Virginia, Minnesota, for permission to reproduce Map E-15 in this book.

Special thanks also to Angela Bauer for her superb work editing the book.

For my cousin, Charles, and my brother-in-law, Theodore: Vietnam veterans who died from prostate cancer due to their exposure to Agent Orange in Vietnam.

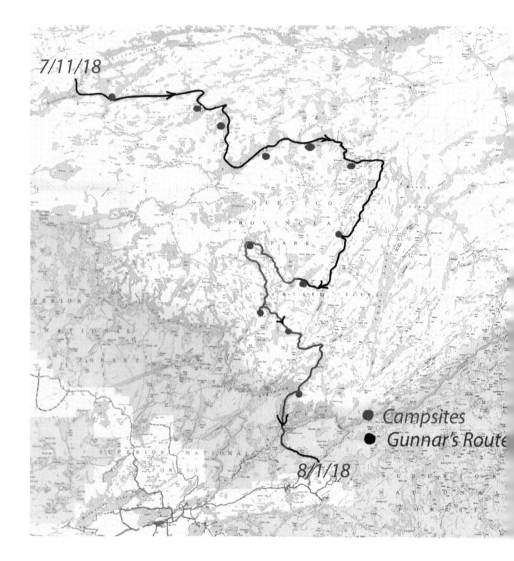

7/11/18

8/1/18

Campsites
Gunnar's Route

W.A. Fisher Map, E-15

THE STORY OF
GUNNAR
HANSEN

———

The Navy F-4 Phantom jets dropped their 500-pound bombs on the enemy position. The sound of the explosions was deafening. What once was a copse of trees and tall grass that provided cover for the Viet Cong was gone, obliterated, along with most of the enemy soldiers. What was left of their bodies littered the ground. The first platoon from Company E, led by 2nd Lieutenant Gunnar Hansen, had taken the brunt of the VC attack, especially the first squad. Hansen was one of the wounded Marines. He lay unconscious, bleeding from a wound in his gut, and near death from blood loss.

Emma

CHAPTER

1

It was still dark outside in the early morning hours of July 11, 2018. Gunnar Hansen was in bed with his wife, Kathleen. He could feel the warmth of her body next to him and could smell her perfume on his pillow. He smiled and turned on his side to look at her, resting peacefully.

"I love you so much, Kathleen," he whispered softly. "I can't imagine my life without you."

The peace of the moment suddenly was shattered by the ringing of his alarm clock. It was 4am and, as he shut off the offending noise and took stock of his surroundings, he realized he had been dreaming. He was all alone in bed except for Emma, his English Springer Spaniel, who had been sleeping at the foot of his bed. When she started barking, it only added to the headache Gunnar felt coming on

"Hush, Emma. Quiet down. I'm awake."

Just then, Gunnar's son Robert poked his head in the room. Emma offered a friendly bark.

"Are you awake, Dad? It's time to get up."

"Don't worry; I'm awake," Gunnar replied, rubbing a hand across his face. "I just had a dream about your mother. I miss her so much." Gunnar gave himself a mental shake to clear his head. "Don't worry. I'll get dressed and meet you and Lucas downstairs. Why don't you take Emma outside to do her thing?"

Gunnar had been anticipating this day — the first day of his "Quetico Canoe Trip of Remembrance," as he called it — for a long time. Ever since Kathleen died in 2008, he had been thinking about and planning a canoe trip in his beloved Quetico Park, where he and Kathleen had spent their honeymoon. They had had so many great adventures there over the years, more than he could count. Kathleen had not only been his wife but his best friend, his lover, his best canoeing bowman. His everything. He hoped, somehow, to reunite with her spiritually as he visited the lakes and campsites they had shared when she was alive. He wasn't sure he could put into words just how important the trip was to him, especially at this point in his life.

He dressed quickly in his canoeing attire, which consisted of his Filson canvas pants, a belt and suspenders, a T-shirt, a flannel shirt, skivvies, wool socks and low-cut hiking shoes with Vibram soles. He also carried a 6-inch Buck knife in a sheath on his right side and a pair of pliers in a sheath on his left side. The pliers had multiple uses, from picking up hot pots from a fire to grasping the mouth of a fish. He used to wear high-top boots, which he preferred because they gave more ankle support, but pressure from the high-tops had started causing pain in his left ankle during the past few years.

Gunnar picked up his personal pack, with his extra clothes and other necessities, from the floor next to his bed and walked downstairs to the kitchen. His oldest son, Lucas, was sitting at the kitchen table drinking coffee and eating a cinnamon roll.

"Good morning, Dad," Lucas said, looking up from his coffee. "How are you this morning?"

"Good," Gunnar replied, setting his pack by the door and settling in across the table from his son. "It's early, but I'm good."

"Let me pour you a cup of java," Lucas said, scooting back his chair and standing to grab a mug from the cabinet. "It will help you wake up."

"You're the one who looks like you could use more sleep," Gunnar said. "But, thanks. Let me try one of those cinnamon rolls, too, please. . . . Where's Robert?"

"He's outside with Emma," Lucas said, placing a mug of coffee in front of his father and returning to the cabinet for a plate. "I think he has most of your gear loaded in the car."

"Great," Gunnar said after swallowing his first sip of coffee and humming appreciatively. "I'll finish my breakfast and then help the two of you tie my canoe to the car."

Gunnar still lived in the same home that he and Kathleen had purchased when they moved to Duluth in 1978 — a two-story, ranch-style house on East Superior Street with a beautiful view of Lake Superior. All five of his kids had been raised there, and that's where he and Kathleen had planned to enjoy their retirement — until her untimely death. Still, he loved living there.

To be honest, he had some reservations about going on a three-week canoe trip, especially since he wasn't feeling well. His recent prostate cancer diagnosis had been upsetting but, after he thought about it, probably not truly unexpected. It had been the *raison d'etre* for going ahead with his trip now. He might be too sick to do it later.

Lucas and Robert lifted the canoe into position on top of the car, and Gunnar helped them anchor it to the roof with some heavy straps before they tied the bow and stern to the bumpers.

Robert whistled for Emma, who had been sniffing around the yard as the men finished packing the car, and then handed Emma over to Gunnar.

"I put all your gear in the trunk, Dad," he said. "I wanted to make sure we have everything — two Duluth packs, two paddles, a life jacket and your fishing rod in its case. Your personal pack can go in the back seat. And we all have our passports, right?"

Emma and Gunnar climbed into the back seat as Robert and Lucas climbed into the front.

"You and Emma just relax," Lucas said, turning to look over his shoulder. "I'll drive now. Robert can take over in Eveleth. It's around 160 miles to Fort Frances from here, so we should be there in about 3 hours."

They planned to clear Canadian Customs at Fort Frances, Ontario, on their way to Beaverhouse Lake, about 75 miles east of Fort Frances on Quetico's northwest edge. That was where Gunnar would start his canoe trip.

The drive was uneventful, but it still was noon by the time Lucas and Robert got the car unloaded and carried Gunnar's gear to the lake. Gunnar carried his canoe, a 38-pound, 16-foot Northstar Northwind Aramid Clear Coat. It was a recent purchase from Pira-gis Northwoods Co. in Ely, a necessity after his realization that his weakened condition meant he couldn't portage anything heavier.

"Boys, this might be the best canoe I've ever had," he said after he set it down. "The yoke pads are really soft and it's well-balanced when I'm carrying it. I know it paddles well, from our trial run last month at Pike Lake in Hermantown. It sure compares well with my Old Town Canadienne, except it's about 30 pounds lighter."

Robert asked Gunnar where he wanted things positioned in the canoe.

"The Duluth packs and Emma each weigh about 40 pounds." Gunnar had done the math at least a dozen times and rattled it off easily. "Emma can help balance the canoe in the bow, along with one Duluth pack next to her and one pack in front of the yoke. I weigh about 180 these days. I'll put my personal Duluth pack, which weighs about 25 pounds, in front of me and my extra paddle and fishing rod case on the bottom of the canoe. Things should balance out and I can always make some adjustments, if necessary."

The Duluth pack is a heavy canvas pack sack with leather straps that's been around since the late 1800s. It was the exclusive pack sack used by the commercial outfitters in the '50s and '60s and at the canoe base when Gunnar was guiding there. It was still his favorite canoe trip pack.

"Dad," Lucas said as he grabbed one of the packs to load into the canoe. "We want you to take a satellite phone."

Gunnar shook his head.

"We've been over this," he said firmly. "Knowing I'm tethered to civilization by a phone of any sort at the bottom of my pack will kill the mood. It'll spoil the feeling of being alone in the wilderness."

It was the same reason he'd decided not to pack a watch.

"Thank you for all your help today, boys," Gunnar said once the canoe was loaded. "I'm really proud of you. You both look more like your mother as you get older. I love you and your sisters. Be sure to give them a big hug. And don't lose that Quetico map I marked for you showing the route of my trip. God willing, I'll finish the trip in three weeks at Sommers Canoe Base on Moose Lake."

Gunnar put on his life jacket, hat and sunglasses and carefully pushed the canoe away from the shore. Then he climbed into the stern and started paddling against a gentle headwind across the lake toward the ranger station on the south shore. Emma rested on the floor of the canoe, in the shade under the bow seat. The rays of the sun, directly overhead and reflecting off the water, were almost blinding. He started to sweat as the heat from the sun bore down on him. Finally on his way, a sense of relief and anxiety stirred within him. Would he be strong enough to complete the trip?

Despite his 73 years, Gunnar still fit most conventional metrics for a handsome man, though his 6'4" frame was thinner than even a year ago. He hadn't shaved in more than a week and his light brown crew cut contrasted with the grey stubble of his forming beard. His facial features hadn't changed much over the years, except maybe for a few more wrinkles extending from the angles of his mouth. He was a soft-spoken, gentle man, and widely respected. That's what people saw when they looked at him.

What they didn't see was how he suffered from the intermittent, dull, aching pain in his groin. They didn't see the catheter in his bladder that allowed him to urinate, or the waves of nausea that he sometimes experienced as a result of the chemotherapy meds he was taking. He felt at times that he was in dark tunnel walking toward a candle that was slowly burning down, like his life, and when the candle lost its flame, he also would lose his. Since he first met Kathleen — Ely, summer 1964 — and fell in love with her, he had never wavered in his feelings for her. He needed to make this trip — and finish it — in spite of how he felt. He prayed each day for that to happen, that the candle's flame would keep burning until he finished his journey.

It wasn't that he was afraid of dying. He truly believed that life on earth is just a brief moment in time, the appetizer before the entrée that is heaven. In spite of the sadness and loneliness he had endured since Kathleen died, and having to deal with prostate cancer, he hadn't lost faith in God. He attended Mass and received Holy Communion every Sunday and often during the week. If anything, his faith was stronger. He thought about the times when he was sure his guardian angel had protected him from harm. He had faith that his guardian angel was watching out for him now.

He would never forget when Kathleen and he were paddling upstream in Kahshahpiwi Creek at Kawnipi Forks in Quetico. He inadvertently had directed the canoe into the fast water pouring into the creek from Kawnipi. They weren't wearing their life jackets. Suddenly, the canoe flipped over, throwing them into the creek. Kathleen kept going under, struggling to keep her head above water. Gunnar finally got her to grab onto the canoe, which was floating next to them. He was starting to tire himself when he felt something holding them up and guiding them to safety to the shore as they held onto the canoe. Kathleen was in shock and shivering from the water, but she was alive. Assured of Kathleen's safety, Gunnar had jumped back into the water to rescue their packs, which were floating downstream, and two paddles. Their cameras and fishing rods had been lost. All of their toilet paper was soaked, along with much of their food, but they had survived.

Another time, Gunnar had been guiding a family of three: a mom and a dad and their 14-year-old son. They had been still fishing for walleyes on the Basswood River, using a rock attached to a rope to anchor the canoes. When the group had tired of that, he untied the rope from the rock and put the rope in the bottom of his canoe before they paddled down to the Lower Basswood Falls portage. Mom and Dad were in one canoe and he and the boy were in the other canoe. You have to be careful at that portage to pull into the shoreline early, before you get too close to the falls. He had landed his canoe and was unloading it when he noticed the parents' canoe was still in the river and going past the portage. Without thinking, Gunnar tied the rope around his chest, jumped in the river and swam out to the canoe to grab it. Someone started pulling on the rope and pulled Gunnar and the boy's parents to safety. When they got to shore, the young boy was sitting down and crying, his face in his hands. He said he had tried to pull on the rope but just wasn't strong enough.

Then there was the time they were on vacation with the kids in Quebec. They were staying at the Chateau Frontenac in Quebec City. Their next stop was Ottawa, Ontario, where they had reservations at the Chateau Laurier, about 270 miles away. They had just driven through Montreal when their car suddenly lost power on the highway about a mile past a service station. After waiting for a few minutes, he was able to get the car started and drive back to the service station to see if the folks there could help him. When he approached the guys at the station, though, they would only speak to him in French and soon ignored him. Gunnar went back to the car to tell Kathleen what had happened. They still had about 100 miles to drive to Ottawa and he was reluctant to keep going, not knowing if the car would break down again. About that time, Gunnar noticed a small blue sedan with Ontario license plates pull into the station for gas. He walked over to the car and talked to the driver, who spoke English. When he explained his predicament, the driver, a young man of about 25, told Gunnar he was on his way to Ottawa and would be happy to have Gunnar follow behind him. He even offered to lead them directly to the hotel. They drove 35 miles an hour all the way to Ottawa, making it in about three hours. When they got to the Chateau Laurier, the young man in the blue sedan drove away before Gunnar could thank him. The man and his car just disappeared. Gunnar found out the next day that his car had a defective water pump, which they were able to get fixed in Ottawa before moving on.

CHAPTER

2

It was December 31, 2017. Gunnar and his family and friends had gathered for a special New Year's Eve party at Northland Country Club. They were celebrating Gunnar's retirement from his law firm, Hansen and Johnson. After nearly 40 years, Gunnar finally had decided to retire. He had started the firm in 1978, when he and Kathleen moved to Duluth. He had just completed eleven years in the Marine Corps, the last four in the Judge Advocate General Division.

"I'm so happy for you, Daddy." Agnes, Gunnar's oldest daughter, punctuated the sentiment with a hug and a kiss to his forehead. "Now that you're retiring, you'll have more free time, more time to travel."

Marie and Ruth, Gunnar's two youngest daughters, also hugged him and kissed him — on his cheek. Robert and Lucas were more reserved but still gave their dad a big hug. Gunnar's five children, all independent adults, loved their dad very much and, like children often do, worried about him. Ever since their mom had died almost 10 years ago, the kids had seemed to worry more about him. Gunnar supposed it was understandable — and he appreciated their concern — but he drew the line at agreeing to the few dates they had tried to arrange for him before giving up with a quiet apology about how he seemed lonely and they were just trying to help, not disrespect their mother's memory. Lately, they'd taken to suggesting he get more rest and that maybe he should see about seeing a doctor for a thorough check-up.

January 2018 was a typical Duluth winter, almost like the one in November 2008, when Kathleen had died. There was a foot of snow on the ground, with more falling almost every day. Lucas and Agnes had stopped by to check on Gunnar near the end of January, after the latest snowstorm.

After cleaning off the new snow from the driveway, they had ordered pizzas from Sammy's Pizzeria in Lakeside and gathered around the fireplace in the living room with Gunnar to enjoy the pizza with his favorite St. Paul brew, Summit Pale Ale.

"Thanks for clearing the drive," Gunnar said as they were settling in. "I was planning to make a trip to the grocery store, but I hadn't gotten around to clearing the drive myself. So, I'm glad you came by. And not just because you saved me the workout. I'm happy to see you both."

After a few minutes of enjoying their food in relative silence, Gunnar found himself telling them that he had made an appointment to see Dan Hamilton at the clinic. Dan was a longtime family friend as well as Gunnar's physician.

"I haven't been feeling well for the past few months, which is one of the reasons I decided to retire," he said. "I've been putting off calling Dan, but I'm not feeling any better, even without pouring all my energy into work."

"Daddy, you should have said something sooner," Agnes jumped in reproachfully. "Is it just that you're tired, or is there more to it?"

"Well, I have discomfort in my lower abdomen," Gunnar said. He wasn't sure he wanted to share all of the details with his children, but Agnes was a nurse anesthetist at St. Benedict's, the hospital affiliated with the clinic. He knew she wouldn't stop pushing until she had the full story. "I'm wondering if it's related to my prostate, since I'm also having trouble urinating."

"What kind of trouble?" Lucas asked.

"I have trouble starting and it sometimes looks like there's blood in it," Gunnar admitted, bracing for Agnes' reaction.

"Oh, Daddy," she started. "Those symptoms can mean a lot of things but, yes, they're often a sign of a prostate problem. How many times have you told us you were exposed to Agent Orange in Vietnam? And how many of your fellow veterans went on to develop prostate cancer? Have you forgotten cousin Chuck? Or Uncle Antonio's brother-in-law, Ted? They were both exposed to Agent Orange. And both died last year of prostate cancer."

"When is your appointment with Dr. Hamilton?" Lucas asked.

"It's February 12th," Gunnar replied. "He won't be back from his vacation in Florida until the 10th. I'm sorry, kids. I didn't mean not to tell you, but you both have a lot going on and I just didn't want to burden you with anything, at least until I had a chance to meet with Dan and see what he says."

Agnes and Lucas agreed that one or both of them would go with Gunnar to his appointment. Agnes said she also would contact Robert, Marie and Ruth and update them. Gunnar didn't say much about all of their planning, but he felt better after they left. Actually, he knew his kids would always be there for him, which is one reason he had been able to survive the past nine years without Kathleen by his side. He was pretty sure that whatever was making him lose weight and generally feel not good was somehow related to his Agent Orange exposure. The herbicide had been sprayed over much of South Vietnam, especially along the Ho Chi Minh Trail, to kill the vegetation. The problem was, Agent Orange contains dioxin, which is extremely carcinogenic, and the Veterans Administration finally and officially had recognized its detrimental effects in the early 1990s. Along with prostate cancer, Agent Orange was implicated in cases of coronary artery disease, leukemia, lymphoma, multiple myeloma, sarcomas and Hodgkin's disease.

Gunnar had already decided that, no matter what was causing his symptoms, he was going to fight it all the way. His folks had taught him that principle when he was growing up. Confront the monster rather than running away. You may not always win the battle, but you won't lose, either; you'll still have your self-respect.

His beautiful, Norwegian mother, Marie, had put that theory into practice when she stood up to her prejudiced Lutheran father and married Charlie, a Roman Catholic. Her father had never spoken to her again. While it was a sorrow she had endured until she died, Marie hadn't regretted her choice, and Gunnar's parents had created a loving home.

Gunnar missed his folks, who had passed away years ago, but he was still close to his brother, Antonio, and his sisters, Anna and Sarah. He made a mental note to call them after his doctor appointment.

CHAPTER

3

———————

Dan Hamilton's office was on the fourth floor of the Northeast Minnesota Medical Clinic, with a view of Lake Superior to the east. Dan was one of the clinic's senior physicians and chairman of its General Surgery Department, having started there two years after it was built in 1971 and sticking around despite the upheaval of the 2010 remodel. Now in his mid-70s, Dan was starting to show his age, Gunnar had noticed. He was 6 foot tall and around 210 pounds, by Gunnar's estimation, and what hair he had left had gone grey. His nose leaned slightly to the right, the result of an old injury, and the white of his dentures complemented his tan from his recent visit to Florida.

"It's good to see you, Gunnar, and you too, Lucas. What brings you here today?"

"Thanks for seeing me, Dan," Gunnar said with a smile. "I brought Lucas for protection, to make sure you aren't going to hurt me when you examine me."

Dan chuckled. "You always have been a big baby when it comes to doctors, Gunnar."

"I know I'm probably a difficult patient, but at least I don't cry when someone tries to take my Jelly Bellies away from me."

"Touche. I love Jelly Bellies," Dan replied with an easy grin before turning serious. "So, Gunnar, what's going on? The last time I saw you was at your wonderful retirement and New Year's Eve party at Northland. I have to tell you that it was one of the best New Year's Eve parties I've ever attended."

"I'm really glad you and Margaret could be there," Gunnar said sincerely. "You are one of my best friends, despite your jelly bean compulsion." Gunnar paused, grateful for Dan and Lucas' polite laughter as he took a deep breath to steel himself for his admission. "I haven't been feeling well for a while now, and I'm having trouble urinating. I have a good appetite, but I've still lost some weight. In all honesty, I'm worried that my exposure to Agent Orange in Vietnam has finally caught up to me and is affecting my prostate."

Dan's nurse had already checked Gunnar's blood pressure, pulse and weight, so Dan reviewed Gunnar's chart and did a thorough physical exam. When he finished, he sat down and talked to Gunnar and Lucas.

"Everything looks good," he said. "Except you've lost 9 pounds since I checked you a year ago and your prostate gland is enlarged. I'm very concerned, like you, that the problem is your prostate gland. I'm going to order some blood tests and refer you to Dr. David Lister at the VA hospital down the street. Dr. Lister is on the faculty of the medical school and is chairman of the VA hospital's urology department. He's a friend of mine. He's very experienced and will take good care of you. You should know this but, as a Vietnam veteran, you are entitled to the full benefits of the VA for service-related illnesses such as prostate cancer, if that is what's causing your problems."

Gunnar nodded his understanding. "What tests are you going to order?'

"You need to have a complete blood count, a renal function test and a PSA test," the physician replied. "The PSA test will measure what are called prostate gland antigens that are circulating in your blood. If they are increased, it suggests you may have prostate cancer. That's where Dr. Lister comes in, because the next step would be to do a biopsy of your prostate and possibly some other tests. He will be in charge of making those decisions."

"Thank you, Dan," Gunnar said, standing. "I trust you, so I'll trust Dr. Lister. How long will it take to get an appointment with him?"

"Sit back down," Dan said, motioning at the chair Gunnar had just left. "I'll call over there right now and see if we can get an appointment sometime early next week. The lab reports should be available by then."

After a few minutes on the phone, Dan hung up and turned his attention back to Gunnar.

"He can see you Tuesday, the 20th, at 2 p.m.," he said. "His office is on the second floor of the VA hospital. Why don't you go with him, Lucas, and one of you can call me after you see Dr. Lister."

Daniel Greysolon VA Hospital sits on University Drive, next to the University of Minnesota Duluth Medical School. A large plaque in the hospital lobby tells the story of how the city was named after Daniel Greysolon, Sieur du Luth, a 17th century French explorer who was said to have been the first European to visit the area.

Gunnar and Lucas took the elevator to the second floor and checked in at Dr. Lister's office. After filling out some paperwork, the nurse took Gunnar back to an exam room and recorded his vital signs, much like the start of his appointment with Dan. Dr. Lister arrived a few minutes later. He looked to be about the same age as Dan, but with a full head of brown hair highlighted by some gray areas at his temples. He was only about 5-foot-5 and slightly overweight. His bulbous nose and large, green eyes gave his face a gentle appearance, in spite of the scattered acne scars on his cheeks.

"I'm so happy to meet you, Mr. Hansen," Dr. Lister began. "I have great respect for veterans, especially those — like yourself — who served in Vietnam. I tried desperately to join the Army when

I was younger, but I was rejected. So I went to medical school and have devoted my life to serving veterans through the VA."

"It sounds as if you've served a lot longer than I did, then," Gunnar replied with a smile. "Call me Gunnar."

"Thank you, Gunnar." Dr. Lister said with a nod. "I read Dr. Hamilton's report and have reviewed the lab tests he ordered. I need to reexamine your prostate and then we'll talk. I just want to reassure you that I have treated many Vietnam veterans who were exposed to Agent Orange and developed prostate cancer. I'll do my best to take care of you."

With that said, he asked Lucas to step out of the room and proceeded to examine Gunnar.

A few minutes later, they were finished and Gunnar settled back on the exam table as Dr. Lister peeled off his gloves and sanitized his hands.

"That exam is really uncomfortable," Gunnar said, trying to relieve some of the awkwardness he felt.

"In what way?" Dr. Lister asked. "Is it painful?"

"No, not really." Gunnar thought for a moment. "It always feels weird, but not painful."

"OK, not painful is good," Dr. Lister replied. "No one I've ever met really enjoys a prostate exam. But, I'm sorry to say, they're going to be a necessity going forward, though I'll try to keep how often I do them to a minimum. I know it's uncomfortable, but it's necessary."

His exam finished, Dr. Lister gave Gunnar a moment to get dressed and, when he re-entered the room, Lucas was with him.

"Your PSA level is greater than 40," Dr. Lister said, getting down to details. "This suggests advanced prostate cancer. Your prostate also is enlarged and feels abnormal. We need to go ahead and do a biopsy of your prostate and an MRI of your prostate and bladder. I'm pretty sure the biopsy will be positive, so we're going to go ahead and schedule a PSMA PET scan, too, to determine if the cancer has spread. Once all of the tests are complete and we have a clearer picture of what we're dealing with, we can discuss how best to treat it."

Gunnar agreed to wait to ask questions about treatment until all of his test results were in, but he did ask if there was anything he could do about the trouble he was having urinating.

"The ultrasound we performed today showed a lot of residual urine in your bladder," Dr. Lister said. "Likely a result of your enlarged prostate pressing on your urethra and blocking the flow. We'll set up an appointment for you to come back tomorrow to have a suprapubic catheter inserted. Simply running a catheter through your urethra won't work, because of your narrowed urethra."

His daughter Agnes accompanied Gunnar when Dr. Lister did the procedure and started him on Tamsulosin, a medication to relax his prostate. She also was with him that Friday morning when the transrectal prostate biopsy was done. Even with the local anesthesia, it was painful and Gunnar groused about it to Agnes as she drove him home. He wasn't much happier as the MRI and PET scans were done over the next ten days, already tired of being poked and prodded and realizing it was just the start.

In all, it was a full month from Gunnar's first appointment with Dan until he had an appointment with Dr. Lister to discuss treating what had been confirmed as prostate cancer. Agnes and Lucas went with him.

"How are you doing with the catheter?" Dr. Lister asked.

"It's taken some getting used to," Gunnar admitted, "but I feel a lot better now that I can fully empty my bladder. Not a terrible trade-off."

"I'm happy to hear that," Dr. Lister said. "As I told you when I inserted it, we'll probably need to leave it in place until normal urine flow occurs, and that might be a while. Unfortunately, the biopsy was positive for cancer, a highly aggressive tumor known as a Gleason 8 intraductal variant. The MRI showed the cancer has spread to your bladder, and the lymph nodes in your groin are enlarged. Fortunately, the PSMA PET scan didn't show any evidence that it's spread to the rest of your body. Your bones and lungs are clear. But, because it has spread beyond the prostate, it's considered a Stage 4 cancer."

Dr. Lister paused as Gunnar took a deep breath and reached for Agnes' hand. Even having lived with the possibility since before he made the initial appointment with Dan and knowing the early tests were enough to confirm it, hearing the stark details and severity were another thing entirely. That many tests couldn't all be wrong.

"The three main treatments for prostate cancer are surgery, radiation therapy and chemotherapy or a combination of all three," Dr. Lister continued when Gunnar didn't say anything. "I reviewed your medical history and surgery is not an option for you because of the battlefield injury to your bladder in Vietnam. There likely would be extensive scar tissue present, making surgery very risky. In addition, surgery is contraindicated with involvement of the bladder and groin nodes. I'm going to recommend we treat you with a combination of radiation therapy and chemotherapy. I can't promise it will cure your cancer, though it *is* possible. Cure or not, I'm hoping you have a good response and we can manage it, and your quality of life. But it will take time."

Gunnar, Lucas and Agnes all had questions, and Dr. Lister spent the next hour answering them and making arrangements for Gunnar's radiation therapy to start March 19 at St. Benedict's Hospital.

"Let me start by telling you about the chemotherapy," Dr. Lister said. "I am going to have you start on Lupron. It's not actually a chemotherapy drug but a hormone medication. Prostate cancer cells are stimulated by the male hormone testosterone. Lupron acts by reducing the amount of testosterone in the body, thus reducing stimulation of the cancer cells. Depending on how you respond to radiation and Lupron, I may try the chemotherapy drug Docetaxel later."

Gunnar finished radiation therapy on April 30 and met with Dr. Lister on May 15 for a checkup and another Lupron injection.

"I feel much better after finishing the radiation," Gunnar told him. "How long do I Have to keep taking the Lupron?"

"At least the next few months," Dr. Lister said. "You also need to have another PET scan."

The scan, done on May 21 showed small metastases to Gunnar's lungs and liver. That led to Gunnar receiving his first injection of Docetaxel on May 25, when he also started taking prednisone.

"I have to be upfront with you, Gunnar," Dr. Lister said. "The fact that the cancer has spread to your lungs and liver is not a good sign, especially since it happened while you were getting radiation and Lupron. I want to keep you on Docetaxel injections every three weeks, along with the prednisone. We have to try to arrest the cancer's growth before it kills you."

"I'm planning to take a three-week canoe trip in Quetico Park in July," Gunnar said. "It's important that I go. Is taking this medication going to prevent that?"

"It isn't going to make for an easy trip but, if you're set on it, we'll do what we can to make it happen for you," Dr. Lister promised. "We'll have to stop the Docetaxel before you leave. Treatment has affected your strength and stamina and likely will continue to do so. But, if you get plenty of rest and try to gain some of your weight back before you leave, it should be do-able. I'll give you another Lupron injection just before you leave on your trip and make an appointment to see you back here on August 14th."

CHAPTER

4

———————

Fredrik and Anna Nipsted emigrated to the United States from Bergen, Norway, in 1908. They settled in Cloquet, Minnesota, a small town about twenty miles west of Duluth. Fredrik started working at the local paper mill and Anna started having children. She had four boys and one daughter, Marie, who was born in 1920. Fredrik and Anna and their children were devout Lutherans. When Marie started dating Charlie Hansen, one of her high school class-mates and a Roman Catholic, her folks were not happy. Marie loved her family and was conflicted as her relationship with Charlie progressed. Charlie, even though he was half Norwegian on his father's side, inherited his Catholicism from his Italian mother. He was a good-looking young man with dark brown hair and an olive complexion, which also came from his mother's side. He was about 5-foot-8 and an outstanding football player on the Cloquet high school team. Marie, on the other hand, was 5-foot-4. A beautiful blonde with an alabaster Norwegian complexion, she was quite a contrast to Charlie.

Charlie and Marie were both good students, though neither had plans to go to college after graduating from high school in 1938. Instead, Marie worked at home with her mother, who was a talented seamstress. Charlie started working at the same paper mill where Marie's father and two of her brothers worked. Marie and Char-lie continued to date, even though it caused a lot of discord in the

Nipsted family. Back in those days, there was a definite anti-Catholic sentiment among some Norwegian Lutherans, and Marie's father had told her flat-out that dating a Catholic was not acceptable. Charlie's family also had reservations about the relationship, telling Charlie that marrying a non-Catholic like Marie was not a good idea. So, over the next couple of years, they maintained a friendship but appeared to have stopped dating, which made both families happy. Truth was, they never really stopped seeing each other; it had become apparent to both of them that they were in love.

Just about the time when their "secret" romance was heating up, World War II was starting. Charlie, like a lot of his friends, signed up for military service. He entered the Army in early 1942 and was assigned to the Army Air Force. He eventually was sent to England in February 1943 as a member of the 445th Bomb Group, which was part of the Eighth Air Force. Because of his size, he was assigned to be a tail gunner in a B-24 Liberator that made regular bombing runs over Germany. During a mission in 1943, his plane was severely damaged by enemy gunfire. He was wounded in both legs, which ended his flying career. When he finally recovered from his wounds in a hospital in England, he was awarded the Purple Heart. He was honorably discharged from the Army in November 1943 and returned home with a mild limp and a cane that helped him to maintain his balance during the next few months.

While he was overseas and writing home often, Charlie had reminded Marie that, even though he loved her, he couldn't marry her if she wasn't Catholic. So, she started taking instruction in the Catholic faith from the local parish priest and officially became a Catholic in September 1943. When Charlie returned home, he resumed working at the paper mill. Marie told him that she had converted. It wasn't long after that, in February 1944, that they were married in a private ceremony.

When her father found out, he disowned Marie and refused to

speak to her again. The tension between Charlie and Marie and the Nipsteds became so unbearable that Charlie quit his job at the paper mill and he and Marie moved to Austin, in southern Minnesota. Austin is the home of the George A. Hormel Co., which processed and sold ham, sausage and other meats. Hormel also created Spam, a cooked pork meat packaged in a neat little can. Introduced in the late 1930s, it gained fame as a staple in C-Rations for troops in World War II.

Charlie got a job at the Hormel packing plant and Marie worked at home as a seamstress. Not long after they moved to Austin, Charlie received a letter from President Roosevelt, advising Charlie that he and his crew members had been awarded the Bronze Star for valor in combat. Even though their plane had been severely damaged by enemy gunfire, the pilot had been able to fly the plane back to their base in England.

They enjoyed living in Austin, away from the Nipsted clan. In some ways, it was a sad time for them, knowing they were separated from Marie's family because of her father's stubborn prejudices. In spite of that, Marie and Charlie were very much in love and were happy together. They made new friends and discovered Austin was a good place for families.

With Charlie's income from his job at Hormel and Marie's seamstress work, they were financially comfortable. Help from the new GI Bill that started in June 1944 allowed them to buy a modest home, and their first child, Gunnar Charles Hansen, was born on March 7, 1945. He was named after his maternal grandfather, Gunnar, and his father, Charles. They had three more children over the next few years: Antonio, named after his paternal grandfather, and two daughters, Anna and Sara. Except for the eleven years when he was on active duty in the Marine Corps, Gunnar lived his entire life in Minnesota. Gunnar attended Pacelli Catholic grade school and high school in Austin and was a very good student. Through the efforts of Brother Frank Clapp, who taught theology and English Literature at Pacelli high school, Gunnar developed a deep sense of love for God. He also discovered Shakespeare, G.K. Chesterton and Dorothy Sayers.

Gunnar matured rather early and was 6-foot-4 by the end of his freshman year. With his bright green eyes, light brown crew cut hair and olive complexion — a gift from his Italian grandmother — he was a handsome young man. He played goalie on the Pacelli hockey team for three years and was a long-distance runner on the track team. By the time he was 16, he had earned the rank of Eagle Scout and took his first wilderness canoe trip with his Scout troop at the Charles L. Sommers Boy Scout Wilderness Canoe Base near Ely, Minnesota. Summer canoe trips became his passion. The 2 million-acre wilderness paradise, which includes Quetico Provincial Park on the Canadian side of the border and the Boundary Waters Canoe Area Wilderness on the Minnesota side, became his summer home.

He made such a good impression on the staff at the canoe base that he was invited to become a guide there. It required a month-long training session known as the *Swamper Program*, but, once it was completed, he would be able to start guiding canoe trips at the base. When his Scout troop took its annual canoe trip in June 1963, he stayed on at the base for another month as a Swamper and then, until he had to leave in mid-August to prepare for college, as a guide for canoe trips, to help make up for a shortage of guides at the base.

The canoe trips Gunnar guided at Sommers Canoe Base all were nine-day trips. Each of the Scouts on the trips had at least earned their First Class Badge. There usually were ten scouts in each group — or crew, as they were called — along with an adult adviser — often the father of one of the Scouts — and the canoe base guide. All of the guides when Gunnar was guiding were men. Their canoes were either Old Town or Seliga 17-foot wooden canoes, except for a few 17-foot Grumman aluminum canoes. The Old Towns, made in Old Town, Maine, had canvas-covered bottoms. The Seligas, made in Ely by Joe Seliga, had fiberglass bottoms.

Those on the trips packed all their food and camping gear in strong canvas packs called Duluth packs. The loaded packs were heavy, especially the food packs, which often weighed 100 pounds at the beginning of a trip, thanks to much of the food being packed in tin cans. Freeze-dried food for camping wasn't readily available at the time. Cans and bottles were finally banned from the BWCAW in 1979. The canoes also were heavy, 85 pounds for the wooden canoes and about 65 pounds for the Grummans.

Gunnar received a number of academic and athletic scholarship offers after he graduated from high school in 1963. He decided to attend the University of Minnesota in the Twin Cities. He played hockey all four years of college, from 1963 to 1967, and majored in business administration, graduating *summa cum laude*. He guided canoe trips at Sommers Canoe Base during the summer of 1963, 1964 and 1965. Bill Rom, who owned Canoe Country Outfitters, the largest outfitter in Ely, offered him a guiding job for the summer of 1966. It paid more money than Sommers so Gunnar accepted. He also returned to guide for Canoe Country in the summer of 1967. It was during the summer of 1964 at Sommers that Gunnar's life took a new direction. Of course, he didn't know it at the time. He was so wrapped up in being a canoe guide that he didn't realize what was happening to him.

Gunnar was relaxing in the guide's quarters, the TeePee, while waiting for the rest of the guides who were going into Ely for the evening. He had returned to the base the previous day, June 23, after an arduous nine-day Quetico trip. He hoped to meet with his friend and college hockey teammate, Jim Drexler, who was working that summer at Olson Bay Resort on Shagawa Lake, just west of Ely.

Gunnar was getting restless and yelled to no one in particular,

"Where is everyone? Come on, let's get the show on the road. It's almost 6 o'clock."

Sandy Bridges, who also had returned from a canoe trip the day before, responded to Gunnar's plea in his distinctive Arkansas drawl. "Sorry to be late. I'm ready. I'll grab Barry and Jay and meet you in the parking lot in 10 minutes."

One tradition of being a guide at the canoe base was that you had a couple of days off to rest after each canoe trip. The day after returning from a trip, guides typically were free for the evening to drive 20 miles — over possibly the worst road in northeastern Minnesota, the serpentine, gravel-covered but still usually muddy and pothole-marred Fernberg Road — into Ely for a hamburger, shake and fries at Vertin's Restaurant or a pizza at the Maid-Rite Cafe on Sheridan Street. After, they would walk down the street to Dee's Bar for a couple of beers and to, hopefully, meet some girls. About midnight they'd all load up for the drive back to the canoe base. (They kept the car windows open in case the bumpy ride didn't sit well with all the beer in their bellies.)

Gunnar was different. He loved to go to Vertin's for a burger, fries and shake, but then he would hang around there and play the latest hit songs on the jukebox, two songs for a quarter. Gunnar was listening to the latest song from The Beatles, his eyes closed as he hummed along, when Jim Drexler slid into the booth across from him. Gunnar had just completed his freshman year at the University of Minnesota when he arrived in Ely in June 1964 to start guiding. In addition to being a goalie on the college hockey team, he was an avid card player, especially bridge. He and Jim had organized a college bridge club that met every week or so. Thanks to his folks, Gunnar knew a number of card games, including cribbage and bridge, the latter of which was very popular on most college campuses at that time. That was thanks to bridge player and writer Charles Goren.

"Jim! It's great to see you," Gunnar said in greeting. "I was wondering if I'd see you tonight. How are you?"

"Hey, Gunnar, good to see you, too," Jim said, sliding into the booth across from Gunnar. "I'm doing okay. The Olson family — they own the resort — are really neat folks. It's pretty busy. Among other things, I take care of the boat dock and the boats and motors. Mr. Olson also has me take some of the guests day fishing on the lake. He knows where all the walleye holes are, so I just run the boat to the hot spots and the guests do the rest. They tip pretty well, too."

"That sounds great, Jim. Are you hungry? Order something, if you want. Then we can grab a beer across the street at the Yugoslav National Home Bar. They don't ask for IDs and they know me, so we won't get turned down. It's quiet there, as opposed to Dee's Bar. I think the guys I came in with tonight are hoping they can connect with some of the gals who frequent Dee's, but that's not for me. It'd be nice to have a girl, but I'm not sure the girls who hang out at Dee's are my type."

Jim agreed with Gunnar that the quieter bar seemed more his style, too.

"Speaking of girls, the Olsons have a daughter, Ingrid," Jim said. "She works at the resort as a housekeeper. She and I have become good friends, though it's strictly platonic."

"Hold on, Jim. Don't give me that platonic stuff. She may say she's just a friend, but watch your back. If she finds you attractive, Plato may be ambushed by Cupid. What else can you tell me about her, 'Mr. Platonic'?"

"Don't jump to conclusions, Gunnar," Jim chastised. "I just met her. Besides being a real looker with a great build, she's smart as a whip. You should see her in a swimming suit!"

"What kind of swimming suit, Jim? One that fits in your back pocket?"

"Give me a break, Gunnar," Jim replied, starting to sound a bit put out by Gunnar's teasing. "When you meet her, you can come to your own conclusions. Anyway, she just finished her freshman year at St. Thomas in St. Paul and she's a bridge nut. Can you believe it? It sounds like she and her friends at St. Thomas spend most of their time playing bridge. I told her about our bridge club at the U and she asked me if I knew any other guys around this summer who play bridge. Apparently, there are a number of Ely girls who are home from college for the summer who would like to get a group together to play bridge with some guys."

"Sounds like a setup, Jim," Gunnar laughed. "But it might be fun. I would be interested and I know some of the guides at the canoe base are bridge fanatics. I think they're pretty good. They asked me to join them a couple of times for games, but I couldn't because I was either on a canoe trip or they were; we're never at the base at the same time. The problem is trying to find a time when we could all get together."

"Let me talk to Ingrid and you talk to the guys at the canoe base," Jim replied. "If she can get three other girls, and you can get a couple of other guides, we'll have four couples, which would be perfect for two bridge tables."

"I think I can get my schedule adjusted so the other guides and I can be free, maybe on a Saturday night in July," Gunnar said after a moment of running through the guides' schedule in his mind. "I leave on another guiding trip on June 26th and will be back at the base on July 4th. I may have another trip in early July, but July 18th could work. We also need to find a place to have the bridge party."

"Let me work on that," Jim said. "Call me when you get back on the 4th and we'll finalize arrangements. Now, how about heading over to the Yugoslav Home Bar?"

5

Gunnar and his crew of Scouts from his latest guiding job returned to the canoe base on the afternoon of July 4. It had been a good trip to Quetico's Kawnipi Lake, where they had great walleye fishing. He finally was able to call Jim the following day.

"Hi, Jim," he began. "Can you hear me okay? I'm calling from the base office phone."

"Hi, Gunnar," Jim replied. "There's a bit of static on my end, but I think I can hear you okay. Did you have a good trip?"

"Yes, it was a good trip. Got back late yesterday afternoon. I have another trip scheduled in two days but I'll be back from that on the 15th. The two guides who play bridge are on the same schedule."

"So July 18th will work for the party?"

"Yes, having the party on July 18th sounds good," Gunnar replied. "I'm coming into Ely tonight. Can you meet me at Vertine's about 8? We can talk more then and avoid this bad phone connection."

"Okay," Jim agreed. "I'll see you tonight. Goodbye."

Ingrid Olson was all Jim had said about her and more. She was a lovely young lady with beautiful blond hair that just touched her shoulders. Gunnar suspected Jim already was pretty far gone on her, and she on Jim, even if Jim hadn't yet realized it.

"I'm so happy to meet you, Ingrid," Gunnar said with a smile.

"And I'm happy to meet you, Gunnar," Ingrid replied. "Jim told me you're the goalie on the hockey team at the U, and that you guys started a bridge club, too. I'm impressed."

"Thanks," Gunnar grinned at her sincerity. "I'm excited about the bridge party. My friends Dave and Maynard, who also are guides at the canoe base, are excited, too. Have you found a place where we can have the party?"

"Yes, and three of my girlfriends who are bridge enthusiasts are anxious to get together. Kathleen Andersson has agreed to let us use her family cabin on Fall Lake, and Mary and Ellen, the other two girls, and Kathleen, have already gotten together to plan the party."

"The girls are talking about making a salad and a cheese and crackers tray with apple pie for dessert," Jim said. "We guys can barbecue steaks and provide beer and soda. Does that sound okay, Gunnar?"

"Sounds good, Jim. Maynard has a car, so we'll plan to drive into Ely about noon on the 18th and meet you and Ingrid here at Vertine's. Then we can go grocery shopping and follow you out to the cabin on Fall Lake."

When Gunnar finally met Kathleen, Mary and Ellen at the Fall Lake cabin, his world changed. He had never felt that way before. There was something about them that he hadn't felt when he met Ingrid two weeks before. It was like a part of his psyche had been asleep and was now awake. At first, he thought maybe it was a pheromone from one of the girls, like the ones that attract honey bees. But when Mary and Ellen came outside while he was grilling the steaks, the feeling wasn't there. Later, when he was helping Kathleen put a Frank Sinatra record on her Victrola, it was as if a magnet was pulling him toward her. Frankly, the intensity was kind of scary. When Frank began singing the Jimmy Van Heusen-Sammy Cahn song *The Tender Trap*, it freaked him out.

Needless to say, the party was a great success. They managed to finish the case of beer before the gathering broke up about 10 p.m., and Gunnar was bewildered by the unexpected attraction he felt for Kathleen. Everyone had such a good time, they managed to get together again a month later, before they all had to pack up to head back to school. Gunnar and Jim were busy with hockey practice and their studies, but they continued their bridge games. Kathleen Andersson also joined their bridge club and she and Gunnar started dating.

CHAPTER

6

Kathleen Emma Andersson was born in Ely on April 17, 1945, the first child of Mary Kathleen and Lucas. When she first met Gunnar in 1964, she had just completed her freshman year in the U's pre-med program. She was a very comely woman with long blond hair and a fair complexion. Standing 5-foot-10 in her stocking feet, she was taller than her two younger sisters, Elsa and Agnes. She was active in dog sledding and skiing in the winter, including competing in ski jumping on Ely's 35-meter ski jump. She was on the swim and basketball teams in high school, along with being an excellent student. Family canoe trips and walleye fishing, which she learned from Don Beland, a popular canoe guide and a friend of the Andersson family, rounded out her summers.

Gunnar returned to guide at Sommers during the summer of 1965. He managed to get together with Kathleen for a few dates. But between her job working as an aid at the Ely Bloomenson Hospital and his guiding schedule at the canoe base, their time together was limited. On one of their dates, Kathleen wanted to stop by Canoe Country Outfitters and introduce Gunnar to Bill Rom, who was looking to hire new guides. Gunnar and Bill liked each other as soon as they met and Gunnar was hired to start working for Bill the following summer. That strange attraction to Kathleen that Gunnar noted at the bridge party in 1964 had matured into a friendship and love. Kathleen was a regular in Gunnar and Jim's bridge group at the U and, yes, Gunnar fell into her "tender trap" — and loved every minute of it. They came to an understanding at the beginning of their romance. Kissing and hugging were acceptable but they both wanted to wait until they were married to go any further. Despite premarital sex being commonplace at the university — and everywhere, for that matter — they didn't see how having sex at that point in their relationship would do anything to strengthen the love they already felt. Agreeing on that didn't necessarily make waiting any easier. They prayed a lot and attended Mass frequently to bolster their determination.

Gunnar bought a used VW Beetle in May 1966, just before the semester ended. He drove to Ely, arriving there on the afternoon of June 6 to start his new job at Canoe Country Outfitters. Bill Rom was in the store and smiled when Gunnar walked in.

"I'm happy to see you, Gunnar," Bill said. "It looks like we're going to have a busy summer. I already have a lot of reservations for canoe trips and half of the groups want a guide. I talked to Anton and Marie Gornik, who live over on Chapman Street, and they have a bedroom in their house that you can rent for the summer. Why don't you get settled in and I'll see you back here in the morning for work?"

"Thanks, Bill," Gunnar said. "I'm happy to be here. I'm supposed to have dinner tonight with Kathleen. I'll head over to the Gorniks' first and I'll see you in the morning."

Before leaving the shop, Gunnar borrowed the office phone and called Kathleen.

"Hi, love," he said. "I just got to Ely and stopped by CCO to check with Bill. Are we still having dinner tonight?"

"Oh, hi, Gunnar," Kathleen responded. "I'm glad you made it. And glad you called. My dad wants to have a cookout. He's going to barbecue some steaks and sweet corn on the grill and Mom made potato salad and a cherry pie. Why don't you come over and we can have dinner here and enjoy a glass of wine. I'm looking forward to our summer together."

Gunnar guided eight canoe trips during the summer of 1966. He helped out at CCO's retail store whenever Bill and Barb — Mrs. Rom — were away. Even though they were both busy, Kathleen and he managed to take a few day trips to nearby lakes using the Andersson family canoe, a 17-foot Seliga. Gunnar had befriended Joe Seliga when he worked at the canoe base and they had become good friends. Gunnar enjoyed watching Joe build his beautiful wooden canoes, now with canvas bottoms, in his garage behind his home on Pattison Street. It had been a good summer for Gunnar and Kathleen. He and Kathleen also were able to get some bridge time in with Jim and Ingrid, and the occasional canoe day trips to Basswood Lake were a welcome diversion.

"Bill asked me to come back next summer to guide again and I told him I'd be back right after graduation," Gunnar said, taking Kathleen's hand in his. "I'm not sure what I'll do after that. A lot of guys are getting drafted for duty in Vietnam. I'm considering joining the Marine Corps. I don't want to be drafted."

Gunnar and Kathleen graduated from the U in May 1967. Kathleen had always wanted to be a doctor and her prayers were answered when she was accepted to the University of Minnesota's medical school starting in fall 1967. Gunnar followed through on his plan to join the Marine Corps. He met with a recruiter, Staff Sergeant Mark Jones, and signed up for four years. He was promised a $10,000 cash bonus when he finished boot camp, because he was a college graduate.

He worked out a deal with Sergeant Jones to spend the summer in Ely, guiding for CCO, before reporting for duty on September 1, 1967. He spent the next 13 weeks in basic training at the Marine Corps Recruit Depot in San Diego, where he earned the rank of private first class. He then moved to the Second Infantry Training Regiment at Camp Pendleton for six weeks before spending another three weeks in final staging at Camp Horno ahead of deploying to Vietnam.

7

The Ranger Station was on the south shore of Beaverhouse Lake. It was nestled in a stand of tall, white pines about 30 meters back from the white, sandy beach. A narrow wooden dock protruded about 10 meters from the shore, connected to a gravel path that led to the front door of the cabin. The ranger's 16-foot Lund boat with its 20-horsepower Mercury motor was tied to the dock. Gunnar landed his canoe on the sandy beach next to the dock and he and Emma followed the path to the cabin.

A young man wearing a park ranger's uniform was standing by the door and greeted Gunnar as he approached. "Hello, welcome to Quetico Park. I'm Jordan Johnson."

"Good afternoon," Gunnar replied. "I'm Gunnar Hansen, and this is my dog, Emma. I need to get a travel permit and a fishing license. And cool down for a bit. The sun is pretty hot today."

"Well, come on into the cabin, where it's cooler," the park ranger said. "I just made some iced tea, if you would like a cold drink. It's been pretty warm the past week or so."

"Thanks very much." Gunnar wiped at his forehead as he followed Ranger Johnson inside. "Iced tea would be great. I see you've got a few solar panels set up. Does that provide much 'juice?'"

"Yes and no," Ranger Johnson replied. "Most of the time I have to rely on a propane generator. It stays pretty cool in the cabin with the fans, and the trees provide a lot of shade, which also helps."

Gunnar and the ranger — he asked Gunnar to call him Jordan— chatted for a while. Jordan said he lived in Atikokan, a town of 2,500 people about 20 miles east on Highway 11.

"The name of the town means 'caribou bones' in Ojibway," Jordan said. "The park's headquarters is in Atikokan. The Souris River Canoe Factory also is there."

"I'm familiar with the Souris River company," Gunnar acknowledged. "They make an excellent canoe. In fact, I considered getting one of their solo canoes for my trip but decided to go with the Northstar 16, because it is a little bigger and has two seats."

After he had spent sufficient time cooling down, without lingering so long that it'd put him behind schedule on Day 1, Gunnar paid for his travel permit and fishing license. He also gave Jordan a paper detailing his 21-day route through the park. "I'm going to have to be on my way, Jordan," Gunnar finally said. "Thanks for your hospitality. I want to get to Eden Island in Quetico Lake to set up camp before it gets too late."

"You should be fine at this time of day," Jordan replied.

"Good to know," Gunnar replied. "Oh, a question . . . I'm planning to camp on Russell Lake. I've been through it a few times but I've never fished it."

"I think most folks consider it a pretty good walleye lake," Jordan replied. "But, like a lot of lakes in the Quetico, you probably can find bass and big northern pike, too. I'm not sure how it would be for lake trout."

"Thanks, Jordan," Gunnar said. "Take care; I need to get on my way."

Gunnar struggled on the portage from Beaverhouse to Quetico Lake, even though it was only 200 meters long. It drove home just how out of shape and weak he had become. He decided to adopt the old French Voyageur technique of carrying his gear part way and resting before going on. Grace Lee Nute, in her book, *The Voyageur's*

Highway, described how on long portages, a Voyageur would carry his load to a "place of deposit," where the load was put down and he rested before the next portion of the portage was taken. Even so, Gunnar was fatigued by the time he found a nice sandy beach campsite on the southwest end of the island. It had been a long day for him. The ache in his groin and intermittent waves of nausea added to his discomfort and made him wonder why he had insisted on making this canoe trip, especially by himself. From what Dr. Lister had implied, Gunnar was fighting a losing battle with cancer. But Gunnar's need to be reunited with Kathleen, if only in spirit, surpassed any pain or discomfort he might have to endure. He was determined to finish the trip.

Someone before him had gathered a few rocks together for a makeshift fire pit, and he unloaded his packs from the canoe and placed them next to the rocks before placing his canoe upside down next to the packs. His paddles and rod case were placed on the bottom of the canoe, out of the way, so he wouldn't accidentally step on them. After setting up the two-person "Big Agnes" tent he had purchased from REI, he placed his new self-inflating foam mattress and down sleeping bag inside the tent. Since Quetico campsites didn't have a biffy like the BWCAW's designated campsites did, Gunnar dug a potty hole back in the woods, making sure it was deep enough and could be adequately covered up when he moved on. It was a routine he would continue for the rest of the trip. Emma followed him around as he set up camp and would lick his hand when he occasionally reached down to pet her.

Aside from the unconditional love he had for his children and Kathleen, Gunnar had a special love for Emma. He had gotten her as a puppy six years earlier and had spent a lot of time training her. She was his constant companion. Both he and Kathleen had grown up with dogs in their families. His folks had a big old black Lab named Bruce, a gentle dog that he and his siblings had loved. Bruce died about the time Gunnar left for college and soon was replaced by a border collie also named Bruce. Kathleen and her sisters had sled dogs, because of their interest in mushing. Kathleen and Gunnar didn't have any family dogs until they moved to Duluth, and then it was by chance that they got their first.

One of Kathleen's colleagues at the clinic was called back to active duty in the Army and couldn't take his dog with him. He asked Kathleen if she would take the animal, a 2-year-old English Springer Spaniel. That was in 1981. They decided to take Rosie, even though it would mean more work for them. They had three children by then: Lucas, 7; Agnes, 3; and Robert, 2 months. The kids loved Rosie and she loved them. By the time Rosie died in 1993, at age 14, they had two more children, Marie and Ruth. They found a new dog to replace Rosie, a 3-year-old Springer Spaniel rescue. After the initial adjustment period for the dog and the Hansens, Lizzie acclimated very well and lived until 2007, a year before Kathleen died.

In 2012, Gunnar started looking for another Springer Spaniel. He was lonely and, with the kids gone, he wanted a dog for companionship. He found a reputable breeder in St. Paul who had 8-week-old puppies for sale. There were six puppies in the litter with a mixture of coat colors. He examined each dog, especially its eyes — the gateway to the soul — before choosing a white-and-liver-colored female he named Emma, Kathleen's middle name. With big, floppy ears and a full chest, she was a beautiful dog. At full-size, she weighed 40 pounds and was intelligent, affectionate and a good watch dog. She didn't bark a lot, except when someone or something disturbed her. She also helped to balance the canoe.

Almost all of the food Gunnar packed was freeze-dried to reduce the weight of the Duluth packs. He normally would have taken some fresh vegetables and bread, and he hoped to supplement his diet with fresh-caught walleye. He did pack 30 ounces of vodka in two light-weight flasks, which he planned to mix with lemonade powder on occasion. He was not much of a drinker — an occasional beer at home or a glass of wine on special occasions — but thought some alcohol might help him relax. He was a strict non-smoker, having seen too many people die from the effects of smoking, including his friend Jim Drexler.

CHAPTER

8

———————

His first dinner consisted of freeze-dried chili, rye crisp crackers and some of the lemonade vodka mix. After washing his dishes, he placed the Duluth packs under the upturned canoe and sat on a log to watch the sunset. Venus was shining brightly in the fading orange sky of dusk. He had a thing for Venus, the Evening Star at sunset and the Morning Star at dawn. He thought about the poem he had written years ago for Kathleen, his personal Venus:

"Morning Star, Evening Star, # 2"

"I saw a dazzling, twinkling glow
Amid the pink and yellow light of dawn,
A faithful sentinel showing where to go.
Oh, Morning Star, be it land or sea
You're always there my love,
Shining bright for all to see.

The light is fading in the west.
Looking up, I see you once again,
Dancing there, doing what you do best.
Oh, Evening Star, I love you so.
I long to fold my arms around your waist
And bathe within the brightness of your glow."

One concern in the Quetico and the BWCAW are black bears and their attraction to food packs. Gunnar had never had a problem with a bear in camp going after his food packs, because he followed very specific rules. First, he kept a clean camp and never took food into his tent. For years, he had put his food packs under his canoe at night and then placed pots and pans on the bottom of the upturned canoe. If a bear went after the food packs, it would have to move the canoe, causing the pots to fall off the canoe and creating a noise that should wake everyone up. Once awake, they could yell and throw rocks at the bear to scare him off.

Another method, recommended by Stu Osthoff, was to use a short rope to lash the food packs to the base of a tree next to his tent. If the bear tried to drag a pack into the woods, it would first have to detach the pack, giving Stu time to wake up, catch it in the act and scare it away. Some people like to hang food packs suspended in the air from a tree branch, but Gunnar didn't endorse it. For one thing, it was a lot of work. For another, bears have been known to climb trees and go after the pack.

Another method, promoted by Cliff Jacobson in his 1995 book *Boundary Waters Canoe Camping with Style*, was to place food packs far back in the woods, on the ground but off the beaten path. The idea was the hope the bear simply wouldn't find the packs. Gunnar *definitely* DID NOT recommend that. Bears are smart and have an incredible sense of smell. Following that approach is like putting a welcome sign on the pack for the bear: "I'm a food pack. Help yourself!"

Gunnar also never stayed in a campsite that appeared to be overused or dirty. This was more of a problem with some of the designated campsites in the BWCAW, and he always avoided them. Following that rule alone probably reduced the chance of a bear invading his camp by 95%. Having a can of bear spray available is also a good idea.

It still was warm outside from the heat of the day and the mosquitoes were starting to bother Gunnar. After emptying the urine bag attached to his leg, he and Emma climbed into the tent. Gunnar relaxed on his sleeping bag, using his life jacket as a pillow. He read for a few minutes from the Bible that Kathleen had given to him when he joined the Marine Corps in 1967. He tried to pray the rosary each night, a habit he had begun as a young boy with his mom and dad. He was a strong believer in the power of prayer.

The familiar call of the loons on the lake outside his tent blended with his memories of life in Duluth with Kathleen and her unexpected death. The memory of that time was as clear now as when it actually occurred.

CHAPTER

9

It was July 1978. Gunnar had just been discharged from the Marine Judge Advocate General Corps. Kathleen had finished her ear, nose and throat residency and joined the Northeast Minnesota Medical Clinic in Duluth. They had two children, Lucas, 4; and Agnes, 2 months. The only people they knew in Duluth at the time were Gunnar's old classmate from college, Jim Drexler, and his wife, Ingrid; together the two couples made a bridge foursome. Jim, a radiologist at St. Benedict Medical Center told Gunnar and Kathleen about a nice home for sale on East Superior Street, and the couple eventually purchased it for $70,000. It seemed a lot to pay at the time, but it proved to be the perfect home for their growing family, especially when three more children soon came along: Robert in 1981, Marie in 1983 and Ruth in 1986.

"Ingrid and I are really happy that you and Kathleen decided to settle in Duluth," Jim told Gunnar. "I thought for some reason that you might end up in the Twin Cities. But Duluth is my hometown and a wonderful place to raise a family."

"Well, I completed my obligation to the Corps and Kathleen finished her fellowship," Gunnar said. "We wanted to be close to our folks in Minnesota, but we didn't want to live in the big city. We both went to college and post-grad there but wanted to get back to a smaller community. Duluth seemed to be a good compromise, and the clinic made her a job offer she couldn't refuse. We're both excited about living on the shore of Lake Superior, something we have dreamed about for a long time. And Duluth is closer to canoe country."

They were sitting in the living room of their new home, drinking coffee and watching the sunrise over Lake Superior. It was Saturday morning, a week after they had said goodbye to the moving van. They didn't have a lot of furniture so one of their projects was to visit the local Ethan Allen store later that day. One of the things Gunnar could never understand about Kathleen was her penchant for antiques. She had come home one time with a car full of kids and old lamps, picture frames, chairs and a box full of what looked to Gunnar like junk she said she found at a local "antique store." There were some other things she had wanted to buy, but she had run out of room in the car.

"Gunnar, my dear, I am so happy we have finally settled down in our own home." Kathleen smiled and gave Gunnar a kiss. "Hopefully, we can find someone who can help care for the children. We'll probably need a full-time nanny, one who may need to live with us."

"Things will work out," Gunnar replied. "Talk to Jim and Ingrid. They may know of someone." He chuckled. "How are you doing at the clinic? When do you start seeing patients?"

"I actually have patients scheduled for next week," she replied. "Until I get established, I'll likely be doing a lot of general ENT — you know, tonsils and adenoids, ear tubes, nose bleeds. Joe Leek said he was going to refer all of his ear cases to me. Up until now, he's been doing the bulk of the mastoidectomies and stapedectomies, but he wants to cut back and get more involved with clinic administration. I told Joe when I agreed to come here that I didn't want to do head and neck surgery or facial trauma."

"You'll do fine, Kathleen," Gunnar reassured her. "Just go slow at first, until you find your groove."

Every time Gunnar looked at Kathleen, he thanked God for

bringing them together. But he noticed the stress of medical school and seven years of post-graduate training, plus childbirth, had begun to take its toll. She was starting to develop lines in her forehead and there were scattered strands of gray in her long, blonde, usually perfectly coiffed hair.

In spite of her busy schedule at the clinic, Kathleen's main focus in life was her family. They both adjusted their schedules so they could all be together as much as possible. Family vacations to the various national parks, plus at least one canoe trip each summer — especially as the children got older — were a great success. On a 1990 trip to Kitty Hawk and the Outer Banks of North Carolina, they chartered a boat and went fishing in the Gulf Stream. Except for 4-year-old Ruth and 9-year-old Robert, both of whom got seasick, they had a great time and Kathleen landed a 9-foot sailfish. Probably the highlight of all of their vacations came in 1995, when they attended the Dietrich von Hildebrand Roman Forum at Gardone Riviera, Italy. They stayed at a first-class hotel on the shore of Lake Garda. Lucas and Agnes attended most of the daily presentations with Kathleen and Gunnar and they all went to the traditional Mass each day. Robert, Marie and Ruth spent most of their time on the beach with the nanny. Highlights of the trip included day trips to Venice and Padua, a boat ride on Lake Garda and a bus ride to visit Trento, in northern Italy.

The years passed by quickly. Kathleen's otology practice developed far beyond initial expectations. People came from far and near to be evaluated by her. She was recognized as an expert ear surgeon and the clinic eventually had to hire another otologist to accommodate all the patients. In April 2008, as Kathleen's 30th year at the clinic was drawing near, Gunnar talked to her about retiring so they could spend more time together. He planned to retire from his law firm, too. As it turned out, she did retire but not by choice.

It was Monday morning, May 19, 2008, when she realized

something was wrong with her left breast. Kathleen and one of her orthopedic surgeon friends, Dr. Ann Morris, were changing into their scrubs prior to starting their surgery schedule, and Kathleen was having trouble adjusting her bra.

"Kathleen?" Ann began. "Are you okay? I can't help but notice you're struggling. Your left breast is unusually red and it looks swollen. Is it sore?"

"It's been bothering me for a few weeks," Kathleen admitted. "Sore and red around the nipple. My bra seems tighter on the left side, too. But I've been busy seeing patients and helping Ruth — our youngest daughter — plan her upcoming wedding. I haven't had time to do anything about it."

"You need to see one of the general surgeons," Ann said.

"You're right," Kathleen acknowledged. "Thanks for the nudge. I'll make an appointment with Dan — Dr. Hamilton — and talk to Gunnar tonight."

She made an appointment with Dr. Hamilton for the following day and told Gunnar that night. His first reaction was to pull her into his arms, hold her gently and kiss her.

"I'm worried, Gunnar."

"Let's not worry until we know there's something to worry about," he replied, running a soothing hand up her back. "Dan will know what it is and what to do. For now, how about we go to North-land for dinner and a glass of wine? You've had a busy day."

"That sounds nice," Kathleen said, pulling back to give Gunnar a small smile.

"I love you, Kathleen," he said. "Whatever it is, we'll get through it. Go freshen up . . . and try not to worry."

Dr. Dan Hamilton was a general surgeon at the clinic. He specialized in breast cancer and colon/rectal surgery and, along with being a family friend, had an excellent reputation.

Kathleen canceled her office appointments for the day and she and Gunnar met with Dan late Tuesday afternoon. Despite Dan's professional demeanor, Gunnar could tell his friend was upset after finishing Kathleen's exam.

"Kathleen, I'm very concerned that the swelling and tenderness in your breast might be what is called 'inflammatory breast cancer.' We'll need to do some blood tests, a mammogram and an ultrasound, along with a biopsy to confirm a diagnosis. I also want you to have a chest x-ray."

Kathleen had a lot of questions and Dan took some time to go over everything with her.

"I've seen a number of IBC cases over the years," he explained. "Though it's still considered a rare form of breast cancer. Aggressive, too. Early detection is important."

"My last mammogram was just five months ago," Kathleen said. "Everything came back normal."

"Then we'll take that as a positive for now," Dan said.

Kathleen had a full surgery schedule the next morning and patients to see in her office that afternoon. She visited the hospital laboratory between cases for the blood tests Dan had ordered. He scheduled her mammogram and ultrasound for Thursday morning and planned a biopsy of her breast on Friday morning in his office. She was more fatigued than normal by the time she arrived home on Friday afternoon and had a difficult time concentrating on Ruth's wedding plans, which took up most of the weekend. Gunnar and Kathleen had tickets for the symphony on Saturday, after which they went out for a late dinner at their favorite bistro in downtown Duluth, the Pickwick.

Dan called Monday afternoon and set up an appointment for Kathleen — Gunnar was welcome, too — to come to his office on Thursday afternoon, May 29, to review the results of her tests. Dan met them in his private office.

"Kathleen, your chest x-ray was normal, but both the

mammogram and ultrasound were abnormal and consistent with IBC. The biopsy also was positive for IBC and the estrogen and progesterone markers in the biopsy tissue were absent, which usually suggests a more aggressive tumor."

Kathleen suspected from what Dan had said when he first examined her that she had breast cancer but was stunned when Dan reported the severity of the tumor. Gunnar also was taken aback by the news.

"Dan, how could this happen to her?" Gunnar asked. "She has always been very healthy and has never really been sick. You took her gallbladder out a few years ago and she fell once while cross country skiing and broke her arm. The only medications she takes on a regular basis are vitamins and an occasional acetaminophen."

Dan nodded in acknowledgement before trying to reassure them.

"Cancer doesn't really discriminate," he said. "But, even though this is an aggressive tumor, about 40% of patients with IBC survive more than five years after treatment, which is encouraging. I hope this will be true for Kathleen. Meanwhile, it's important to begin treatment as soon as possible. We also need to get a baseline MRI scan now to make sure the tumor hasn't spread to other areas of the body and then we'll repeat the scan before surgery. The initial treatment is chemotherapy, then radiation. It will take about three months to complete. If the tumor responds well — that is, if it appears to have stopped growing and is reduced in size — then I will proceed with surgery, which includes removal of the left breast — a mastectomy — and removal of the lymph nodes in the left armpit."

"Why start with chemo?" Gunnar asked. "Why not start with surgery and remove the tumor?"

"Because of the type of cancer Kathleen has, treating her initially with drugs injected directly into her bloodstream hopefully will destroy any cancer cells that may be circulating in her blood," Dan explained. "Radiation therapy uses very high beams of energy to kill cancer cells in the breast tissue. Surgery is the last step, to remove the diseased tissue that has been sterilized by the preceding treatments. Combining the three treatments means the chance of completely eradicating the tumor is greater."

Dan paused for a moment as Gunnar and Kathleen tried to absorb what was, in context, an overwhelming amount of information., "Because of the side effects of the chemo and radiation, primarily fatigue and weight loss, you'll need to take an extended leave of absence from work, Kathleen. I will make arrangements to get you started on the chemotherapy as soon as possible."

Kathleen began her chemotherapy on June 8, 2008. Dan Hamilton inserted a port under the skin on her upper chest, just below her collarbone, on June 2. The port, a flat plastic bubble with a tube that is inserted into the vein under the collarbone, made it easier to administer intravenous doses of the chemotherapy drug she would receive twice a week for eight weeks. She tolerated the treatment pretty well except for some nausea and vomiting for a day or so after each injection. Her weight dropped from 139 pounds to 109 pounds, mainly because she didn't have much of an appetite. She also lost most of her hair. Still, she started feeling better as soon as the chemo had ended and two weeks later had gained back 8 pounds. Then she started the six-week course of radiation to the left breast. That didn't go as well, and she had to discontinue the treatment after five weeks because of pain and discomfort at the radiation site.

When her treatment started in June, Gunnar took a leave of absence from his law practice and accompanied her to every chemotherapy and radiation treatment she received. Afterwards, he would take her home so she could rest. It was a very difficult time. When she stopped her radiation on September 19, Gunnar called Dan and made a follow-up appointment for Kathleen to see him on the 30th.

The appointment went well. Dan said he was pleased with the response she had from the chemo and radiation, even though she had stopped the radiation early. The breast tumor had gotten much smaller. The next phase of the treatment plan was to do a mastectomy and axillary node dissection. He wanted to wait a month or so to let the skin around the breast heal from the radiation. In the meantime, she needed to try to gain some weight and get plenty of rest and exercise. Gunnar made plans for them to drive up to Ely to their cabin on Burntside Lake for a week or two.

Kathleen had her repeat MRI on October 27. She was feeling more like herself, except for some pain in her left thigh. She had gained 10 more pounds and her hair was growing back. She had even gone trout fishing on Burntside while at the cabin and had a chance to visit with her sisters, who still lived in Ely.

On October 29, her mother's birthday, she received a call from Dr. Hamilton to meet him at his office that afternoon. He directed Kathleen and Gunnar to his private office and told them the scan showed the tumor cells had spread to her lungs, liver and left axilla. There also were hot spots in her pelvic bone and her left thigh bone that suggested tumor cells also had spread to those areas. The metastases ruled out doing the planned surgery. He suggested that another course of chemotherapy might slow down the cancer's growth, but he wasn't optimistic.

Kathleen couldn't bear the thought of more chemo, which would make her sick again and only prolong the inevitable. She told Dan she thought her best treatment option was to spend time with her family and pray for a miracle.

Ruth's wedding went on as planned on November 19, two weeks before Thanksgiving. Gunnar and Kathleen's oldest son, Lucas, had just joined his father's law firm, which made Kathleen very happy. Agnes, who was 30 at the time, was a nurse anesthetist at St. Benedict's. Marie was 25 and a graduate student at the U, working on her master's degree in entomology. Robert, 27, was a civil engineer who worked for a construction company in Madison, Wisconsin. Ruth, the newlywed, was studying to be a chef. They all celebrated Thanksgiving with their parents in Duluth.

A major snowstorm on November 27, Thanksgiving Day, made traveling hazardous, but everyone made it home to help prepare the Thanksgiving dinner. The kids insisted that Kathleen and Gunnar relax, so they sat on the couch and watched the snow swirling around outside. They held hands and Kathleen told Gunnar how happy she was that their family was together. Gunnar put his arms around her and held her gaunt body. It was all he could do to keep from crying, knowing that likely was their last Thanksgiving together.

Kathleen wasn't very hungry at mealtime, but she did eat two pieces of pumpkin pie, her favorite. After dinner, the family gathered in front of the fireplace, enjoying the warmth from the fire.

Kathleen was seated next to Ruth and Ruth's new husband, Jim, when she suddenly started to cough and her breathing became labored. Then she stopped breathing altogether. Ruth quickly laid her on the floor and Agnes started CPR as SOMEONE called 911, only to be told the snowstorm meant an ambulance wasn't going to arrive anytime soon. After about 10 minutes, Lucas took over for Agnes on the CPR, but with no better success.

Everyone was stunned. Kathleen was dead. Agnes thought it might have been a pulmonary embolism, since it was so sudden. Gunnar was devastated but tried his best to hold it together in front of his children, who had just lost their mother. Lucas and Robert gently lifted Kathleen's fragile body and laid it on their bed. Robert was able to drive through the snowstorm to bring Father McCarthy from the cathedral to administer the sacrament of Extreme Unction, the Last rites.

Kathleen was buried in Calvary Cemetery in Duluth.

CHAPTER
10

The warm sunlight beaming through the tent window finally awakened Gunnar on July 12, the second day of his trip. He opened the tent flaps and stepped outside. A simple breakfast of Gene Hicks coffee, cinnamon-raisin instant oatmeal and stewed fruit filled him up. He thought about his old friend, Gene Hicks, as the coffee was brewing. Gene was a fishing guide from Ely who started Gene Hicks Gourmet Coffees in 1999, after he retired from guiding. Gunnar had engaged Gene a number of times in the 1980s for fishing day trips around Ely when the children were younger. He hadn't been in contact with Gene for a while, but he sure enjoyed the coffee.

Quetico Lake — *gwe taa maang* in Ojibway, meaning "sacred land" — has special meaning to the Ojibway, who believe the lake is occupied by "living spirits that have been there since time immemorial." It's a wonderful lake with clear water, lots of sandy beaches and beautiful second-growth red and white pines, birch, aspen and cedar trees scattered along the shoreline.

The second day of Gunnar's trip entailed a 15-mile paddle due east to the Conk Lake portages, then on to Jean Lake, where he planned to camp. The first time he had visited Quetico Lake was in 1964, when he was coming from Jean Lake. He had to battle a fierce head wind on Jean and was wind-bound at the end of the second Conk Lake portage at the west end of Quetico until dusk. Once the wind subsided, he and his crew of Scouts had paddled all the way to Eden Island, their path illuminated by a full moon and millions of sparkling stars. It was a breathtaking experience.

Gunnar's favorite paddle was his Bending Branches Expedition straight shaft model. The Expedition model also was his backup paddle. He liked to paddle on both sides of the canoe so, when his shoulder and arm would tire, he could switch sides and paddle on the opposite side, port or starboard, whatever it might be. He also would have his bowman change sides when he had one. This method allowed his arm and shoulder muscles on one side to rest. He controlled the direction of the canoe and kept it going in a straight line using a combination of a draw stroke and J-stroke that he nicknamed the "slip stroke." He had perfected the technique while guiding at the canoe base.

"Emma, let's take a break here at the Conk Lake portage," Gunnar broke the silence. "You seem like you're getting restless, which means you could probably stand a walk, and I need to empty my urine bag."

Gunnar had planned his route for his canoe trip by picking campsites he had visited with Kathleen. There are two portages from Quetico Lake to Jean Lake via Conk Lake. The first portage from Quetico into Conk is the length of a football field. The portage from Conk to Jean is the length of two football fields. He made three trips on each portage and, even with his lightweight gear, he was pretty worn out when he finished the second portage. He found the campsite on Jean on a point not too far from the portage where he and Kathleen had stayed. The landing was rocky, so he was careful as he stepped out of the canoe into the water, unloaded his gear on the shore and then carried the canoe up to a spot where there was a small fireplace. There was a pile of firewood next to the fireplace and a nice place for the tent. He threw a stick into the lake and Emma jumped in after it, swimming around for a few minutes before retrieving the stick; she managed to give Gunnar a shower when she shook off the water. They sat for a while, resting on the rocky point. A gentle breeze and the late afternoon sun warmed them and dried them off. Gunnar made a pot of coffee and shared a cookie with Emma.

Day 3, July 13, was overcast and he could smell rain in the air. After eating breakfast, Gunnar packed up and headed for the 400-meter portage that would take him to Burntside Lake, where he planned to camp at one of Kathleen's favorite campsites, a pine-covered point with a sandy beach. It rained most of the 2 hours or so that it took him to carry his gear over the muddy, rock-strewn portage, but it was just a gentle mist by the time he set up camp. Carrying the canoe and packs over the portage once again had worn him out.

Someone had built a fireplace and left a small stack of wood next to it. He gathered some beaver wood that had washed up along the shoreline. Beaver wood is aspen, birch or alder that has had the bark stripped off by the beavers. The bark is part of their diet. It's the best wood for cooking fires as it burns cleaner than pine and doesn't spark. If it's available, cedar is also good for firewood.

He boiled water for his dinner of freeze-dried mac and cheese, accompanied by more of his lemonade vodka mix. The food and the appearance, finally, of the sun in the western sky gave him a feeling of contentment. After dinner he heated water in one of his big pots and washed his dishes. After dumping that water in the woods, he heated more water to wash the area where the catheter was protruding from his body and applied a fresh gauze dressing and antibiotic ointment, a ritual he repeated every night. After placing the Duluth packs under his canoe and positioning the pots and pans on the bottom of the upturned canoe, he and Emma crawled into the tent. Daylight was fading and he was tired. He fell asleep listening to the haunting sounds of the loons calling.

The sun was shining when he woke up on Day 4, July 14. This was a layover day and he decided to spend some time going through his packs to check his gear before going fishing. He had a simple cook kit: a 1-quart aluminum pot with a cover and handle, a 2-quart aluminum pot with a cover and handle, a six-cup coffee pot, a 10-inch frying pan and two sets of reusable plastic dinnerware, including two cups. He had another cup that he kept attached to his belt, so he could get a drink of water from the lake while he was paddling. His utensil roll-up kit included two sets of reusable plastic knives, forks and spoons; a long cooking spoon and a long spatula. These were all packed in a nylon cook kit bag along with a 1-quart plastic bottle with a lid and a collapsible 1-gallon bucket. He also had a waterproof ditty bag with dish cleaning supplies, two Zippo lighters with a small can of extra lighter fluid and 20 waterproof matches. His one-burner lightweight propane Coleman stove and three bottles of propane completed his cooking gear. It all seemed to be in fine shape.

"I'm going to brew a pot of coffee, Emma, and I've got some doggie treats for you," he said, tousling the dog's ears. "I need to get a little java in me this morning. Then I think I'll go through all the fishing gear before doing some walleye fishing this evening."

Emma relaxed next to Gunnar as he drank his coffee and munched on some peanut butter and rye crisp crackers. He gave her a dog treat.

When he had finally decided to take his solo canoe trip, he realized he would have to limit how much gear he could take with him, especially his fishing gear. While fishing was not the primary goal of his trip, it certainly was a secondary goal. He realized the trip might be the last time he would be able to enjoy the excitement of fishing in the Quetico. It also wouldn't hurt to supplement his diet with fresh-caught walleye.

First on his list of gear were his two 6.5-foot St. Croix action rods, which had been gifts from his kids on his 65th birthday. One was a light-medium model for bass and walleye, and the other a heavy-medium model for trolling. He took two open-faced spinning reels, a Penn 4300SS and a Pflueger Patriarch, and four spools of line. Two spools were filled with 8-pound test and two with 12-pound test Kast King low-vis braided line. Since live bait wasn't allowed in Quetico Park, the hardest job was trying to decide what lures to take.

Barbless hooks also were required in the park, so he removed the barbs from all of his lures. He decided he was going to concentrate on walleye, northern pike and bass and not spend time fishing for lake trout, which were best caught in May or June. He contacted his friend Stu Osthoff in Ely and asked him what lures he would recommend. Stu sent him a list of his favorites, which included the jointed Rapala Shad Rap 9 and the Shad Rap 7 lures for walleye, along with yellow ball jigs and Gulp! Minnows. For bass, he took Rapala No. 5 Blue Fox Vibrax Spinners, which run deep, and Whopper Ploppers, which are surface lures. His favorite northern pike lure was the Vibrax No. 5. To Stu's recommendations Gunnar added some of his own favorites, including the Rapala Deep Tail Dancer and the Doctor Spoon 285. He also packed titanium leaders, swivels, lead weights, a small wire cutter, a fillet knife and sharpening stone, a Surefire flashlight and an extra battery, 150 feet of rope, a landing net, a combination fish scale and measuring tape, a first aid kit, a fold-up shovel, a BWJ Turbo cut camp saw, a camp axe and four rolls of toilet paper.

Gunnar was an avid fisherman. His love for fishing probably went back to when he was 13 and his family was vacationing at Sha Sha Resort on Rainy Lake near International Falls. His dad had taken Gunnar and his brother, Antonio, fishing on Rainy. Gunnar caught a 12-pound northern pike on a Daredevil with his old Shakespeare rod and spinning reel with a 12-pound test line. They took some pictures before his dad said they had to release the fish. Gunnar was heartbroken but his dad had explained that they didn't plan to eat the fish and he wasn't going to mount it, so it was best to release the fish so someone else could catch it. That's when Gunnar learned about catch and release. He had been a proponent ever since. Kathleen had been a fishing addict. She had an innate sense of where to fish and when was the best time. She had even liked to ice fish when it was 20 degrees below zero.

Gunnar caught 10 nice 15-to 18-inch walleyes when he went fishing near sunset in a spot off the point near his campsite. He used a Shad Rap 7 in about 10 feet of water. He kept two of the fish for supper and released the rest. After filleting the fish back at his campsite, he coated them with a breading mix and fried them in canola oil. Freeze-dried corn and his lemonade vodka mix rounded out the meal. After cleaning everything, he packed up his fishing gear and placed the fish guts on some rocks on the shore for the gulls. With his food packs safely under the canoe, he and Emma went to bed.

CHAPTER

11

An early morning thunderstorm on Day 5, July 15, delayed Gunnar's start to Sturgeon Lake. He hoped his favorite campsite, a large sandy beach point about 4 miles east of the bay where the Jean Creek enters Sturgeon, would be open. It was one of those special places where one could walk into the lake on the sandy bottom until you were neck deep in clear water.

It was midafternoon when he finally reached Sturgeon and paddled toward the campsite in calm water with a gentle tail wind. He was elated to find no one camped there. He had picked up some beaver wood at the last Jean Creek portage, so he had a nice stack of firewood when he got to the campsite. It was a big campsite. There were three fireplaces erected in various locations. Red and white pine trees provided shade and a thick carpet of needles on the sandy soil. He picked a spot on the east end of the point and started setting up camp. As he was doing this, he noticed three Kevlar canoes coming toward him from the east. As they got closer, he could see they had the Sommers Canoe Base logo on the bow of each canoe. He and Emma walked down to the shore to meet them.

"Hello," a young woman in the stern of the lead canoe greeted him. "I'm Bridgett Olson and I'm guiding a group of Scouts from Sommers Canoe Base. We were planning to camp here tonight."

"Hello to you. I'm Gunnar Hansen," Gunnar introduced himself, "and this is my dog, Emma. This is a big campsite. There's plenty of room for all of us, if you folks still want to camp here."

Sitting in the bow of the guide canoe was an older man who looked to be about 50 and apparently was the adult leader of the group. There were three teenage boys in each of the other two canoes. They all looked exhausted. The woman and the man conferred for a minute.

"Thank you very much," Bridgett said. "We'll go ahead and set up camp on the other end of the point."

"Yes, thank you," the man in the bow said. "We're pretty tired, so I think everyone is happy to stop for the day. I'm Jack Riley, by the way." He motioned to one of the other canoes. "I'm with my youngest son and his friends. This is the first canoe trip for all of us and it's been a great experience. We better get going, but maybe we can talk later tonight."

With that introduction, the crew paddled around toward the other side of the point and, after a bit, Gunnar could hear them getting their camp set up. He remembered the days when he was guiding at Sommers. It was a lot of work and a lot of fun but definitely a job for energetic young folks. Gunnar was washing his supper dishes when Bridgett stopped by his camp to thank him for sharing the campsite. She was an attractive woman, about 5-foot-8 and around 140 pounds, in Gunnar's estimate. Her skin was tanned and her blond hair was gathered up in a red ribbon. She invited him to visit their camp later that evening for Kool-Aid and popcorn. It turned out to be a real treat for Gunnar. He met the Scouts, all of whom were from Wichita, Kansas. The older man, Jack Riley, introduced himself again and also thanked Gunnar for sharing the campsite. He mentioned he was a U.S. congressman representing the fourth congressional district in Kansas, which included Wichita.

"Jack, call me Gunnar," Gunnar said. "I'm glad it worked out for you all to camp here. This is one of my favorite campsites, for obvious reasons. I used to be a guide at Sommers back in the '60s. I guided there for three seasons and did some commercial guiding for a couple of years before I joined the Marine Corps. We didn't have girl guides then. Like everything in the world, things have changed a lot."

"Yes, Gunnar," Bridgett said with a smile. "Girl guides are now part of the new Boy Scouts policy. It has worked out just fine. I've been guiding for five years. Before that, I was the assistant base director for three years. I'm not sure how long I'll keep guiding, though. I'm 30 and have a full-time job in the off-season teaching literature at Edgewood Catholic High School in Madison, Wisconsin."

"Well, more power to you, Bridgett," Gunnar replied. "My three daughters have been on many canoe trips, but they were never interested in becoming guides."

"You mentioned you were in the Marine Corps, Gunnar," Jack said. "What do you do now?"

"I live in Duluth. I retired from my law practice in December. Since then I have been diagnosed with prostate cancer and am still on chemotherapy. I have wanted to take this canoe trip for a long time, so I'm finally doing it. This is Day 5 of a planned three-week trip, just me and Emma. My wife, Kathleen, died about 10 years ago and I'm trying to revisit some of our favorite campsites and lakes in the Quetico and do some fishing."

"I'm sorry to hear about the cancer, Gunnar," Jack said. "How are you doing?"

"I'm feeling better," he said, "but I still don't have my strength back. It's been a difficult time but I decided if I don't do this canoe trip now, I may never do it. Anyway, I always feel I'm 'home' when I'm in the Quetico."

"I never knew my dad," Jack said. "He was a Marine, too, and I was just a baby when he was killed in Vietnam in 1970. Mom told me a lot about him, but it's just not the same, if you know what I mean."

Gunnar was quiet for a moment as he let what Jack had said sink in.

"Jack," he finally said. "I was in Vietnam in 1970; my second deployment. My CO then was Captain Jack Riley, who was from Kansas. Could that have been your dad?"

"Seriously?" Jack's eyes grew wide.

"We were in the Que Son mountains, involved with an operation called Imperial Lake," Gunnar supplied. "That's where I was stationed when I was wounded in September 1970."

"Oh, wow." Jack seemed stunned. "That must have been my dad who was your CO. I can't believe I'm talking to someone who knew Dad and was actually with him in Vietnam, here on a wilderness canoe trip."

"That's incredible," Bridgett spoke up.

"I don't believe things happen by 'chance,' but I do believe in forces beyond our understanding that work together with our free will and allow things to happen," Jack said.

"Me, too, Jack," Gunnar agreed. "I have experienced a number of things that have happened during my life that I can't explain."

"How well did you know my dad?," Jack asked. "Could you share with me what you remember about him?"

"I'll be happy to tell you what I remember," Gunnar replied. "I'll have to think about it, though. That was a long time ago. Since it's getting late and I need to hit the sack, let's meet tomorrow morning for coffee at my camp and we can talk then. Thanks for sharing your campfire tonight. I had a great time."

Gunnar was tired as he walked back to his camp with Emma. After doing his usual night time chores, he and Emma curled up in their tent. Gunnar couldn't get over meeting Captain Riley's son here on Sturgeon Lake. It's been almost 48 years since that awful day when Gunnar had almost died in Vietnam. Gunnar's experiences on both of his deployments were like a nightmare that he had tried to forget, and now he was being reminded about it again. He slipped into his sleeping bag but left it unzipped as he rested his head on his life jacket. He drifted into a restless sleep, dreaming about when he went to Vietnam the first time, in 1968.

CHAPTER

12

The Pan Am flight from Los Angeles via Okinawa landed at Da Nang Air Base on February 12, 1968. Gunnar was one of the new recruits — fresh from staging at Horno Base at Camp Pendleton — who were starting a 13-month deployment to Vietnam. They were part of the 1st Marine Division that controlled Da Nang at the time. Gunnar kept asking himself what he had gotten himself into. Frankly, he was too naive at the time to understand the severity of his situation. It was a culture shock from the moment he stepped off the plane. The air was hot and muggy and there seemed to be confusion everywhere. He also had a headache and jet lag. He must have been daydreaming, because he suddenly heard someone yelling at him.

It was Sergeant Jay Williams, Gunnar's squad leader.

"Hey, Hansen, get your ass over here and form up with your squad."

"Yes, sir," Gunnar replied hastily, grabbing his duffle bag before running to fall in where the rest of the guys were standing.

Gunnar's squad joined up with two other squads to form a platoon. Second Lieutenant James Cassidy, Gunnar's platoon commander, introduced himself and got down to business.

"All right, Marines," he barked. "Let's load up in the trucks. We're headed to base camp, where you will be billeted. After chow, we'll have orientation and you'll be given your assignments. We'll all be going on patrol in a couple of days."

That was the beginning of one of the worst years of Gunnar's life, when he didn't know from one day to the next if he'd survive. He initially was part of an infantry battalion engaged in counter insurgency operations. They were sent out on long-range patrols in the foothills south of Da Nang, the so-called Que Son Valley. He was just getting used to his new life, if that's possible in a hell-hole like Vietnam, when his platoon was involved in a serious fire-fight with the Viet Cong, referred to as the VC, in early June, that lasted a day and a half. Sergeant Williams, Gunnar's squad leader, was killed and Second Lieutenant Cassidy was seriously wounded. Gunnar was promoted to lance corporal.

In August, Gunnar's platoon stumbled into an ambush in the area known as Death Valley. His squad was credited with holding off the enemy until air support arrived with 500-pound bombs that created craters in the ground and knocked out your hearing if you were too close to the explosions. A lot of guys were killed or wounded, and Gunnar was given a battlefield promotion to corporal.

Gunnar's battalion mainly had to deal with the VC, South Vietnamese splinter groups whose members sympathized with North Vietnam. They were composed of men and women who dressed in black pajama-like clothes and hid in caves and tunnels or concealed themselves behind bushes and trees, exposing Gunnar and his fellow Marines to the constant threat of death from sniper fire. They also had to contend with booby traps set by the VC.

Punji sticks — sharpened bamboo jammed into pits dug in areas where troops would be walking — were the worst. The holes were covered with branches or grass to conceal them. When stepped on, the covering would collapse and the unsuspecting victim would fall into the pit to be impaled on the sharp bamboo sticks. Sometimes the VC went one further, coating the sticks with feces or poison to make any wound more likely to get infected. They also devised what was referred to as a cartridge trap, a bamboo tube attached to a piece of wood placed in a disguised pit. A live ammo cartridge would be placed in the bamboo tube on top of a nail and, if someone were to step on the bamboo stick, the pressure would push the bullet onto the nail, thus shooting the victim. The bamboo whip trap was another hazard that could suddenly impale the victim with a spike if the tripwire was triggered.

Along with the never-ending heat and humidity, monsoons, bugs, snakes, leeches and a shortage of drinking water, it was almost unbearable. The leeches were particularly obnoxious. They would drop on to a guy from the tall elephant grass and attach to his chest, armpits, groin. Sometimes even his penis. They sucked their host's blood until the host had a chance to get rid of them by applying mosquito repellent. Some men who were attacked by leeches had to be air evacuated to a medical facility.

On more than one occasion Gunnar and his buddies asked themselves why they were fighting. Fighting in Vietnam wasn't like World War II or Korea, where there were defined battle lines. Vietnam was strictly guerrilla warfare. Gunnar was certain he'd never forget how a Navy corpsman saved his life. Gunnar had been in a firefight with the VC while on patrol when his friend, Lance Corporal Tom Wilson, was wounded, bleeding and crying from the pain. Gunnar rushed to help the corpsman who was with Tom and failed to see a VC who had his rifle pointed at Gunnar. Fortunately, the corpsman spotted the man and shot him before the man could fire on Gunnar. Tom died on the battlefield a few minutes later.

Gunnar was transferred in January 1969 to the 3rd Marine Division and was part of Operation Dewey Canyon in the Dakrong Valley in western Quang Tri Province. They crossed into Laos and discovered a large cache of enemy supplies, arms and ammunition.

He was promoted to sergeant on March 1, near the end of his 13-month deployment, and flew back to San Diego from Da Nang Air Base on March 17, 1969. Before he left Vietnam, his CO suggested that Gunnar consider applying for Officer Candidate School when he got back to Camp Pendleton.

Gunnar awoke suddenly. It was still dark out and very quiet. He needed to empty his urine bag — too much Kool-Aid at the Scout camp. Emma followed him out of the tent and walked away from the campsite to do her thing before the two of them settled back into the tent.

"I'm glad you didn't bark; it might wake someone," Gunnar said, patting the dog. "I think I'm going to actually get inside my sleeping bag and zip it up — I'm chilly. You can settle down at my feet and help keep my toes warm."

Still, Gunnar lay awake until dawn. His dream about Vietnam disturbed him, as it often did. He thought about Agent Orange and all the suffering it had caused, his present condition a case in point. He could still hear the familiar noise of the prop planes as they sprayed the liquid poison — almost 20 million gallons over the course of the conflict — over much of the landscape of South Vietnam. While it did its job of defoliating the lush forest landscape that provided concealment and food for the enemy, it fell like rain on Gunnar and his fellow ground troops who were exposed to it. The military called the spraying Operation Ranch Hand and it lasted from January 1962 until May 1975. Along with killing trees and crops, it also contaminated Vietnam's soil and water for eons and, in many ways, was a complete debacle. It made Gunnar think of a quote from 17th century philosopher Francis Bacon: "The remedy is worse than the disease."

CHAPTER

13

———————

Jack Riley walked into Gunnar's camp about midmorning. It was July 16, Day 6 of Gunnar's trip.

"Good morning, Gunnar," he said by way of greeting. "I'm still trying to understand how fate has brought us together in this beautiful place. I don't think I've ever experienced anything as exciting as this canoe trip. The boys all wanted to go swimming and Bridgett is going to act as lifeguard. They're supposed to wear their life jackets most of the time, but I told her it would be safe to swim without them. It's such a beautiful beach."

"It is," Gunnar replied. "I think that's the major attraction for this campsite. That and having room for a lot of tents. Sit down, Jack. I'll pour us a cup of coffee and we can talk about your dad. At least what I can remember from that time."

"That would be great," Jack said with a smile as he settled near the campfire. "I like my coffee black. I really appreciate your doing this, Gunnar. I have talked to some of the men he was with in Vietnam, but none of them could remember much and were kind of reluctant to talk about that time. It must have been brutal over there for you guys."

"Let me put it this way, Jack," Gunnar started his explanation. "I don't know of any Marine who was in the infantry and survived their 13-month deployment who would want to go back for another round. But many of them did have to return a second time. It wasn't any easier the second time around and many of them came home in a body bag."

"Well, I commend you, Gunnar, for your service. Before you tell me what you remember about my dad, let me give you what little background information I have."

Just then, Emma jumped up and ran down to the shore, barking at a group of four large Northstar canoes heading west. The Boundary Waters Journal logo was painted on the bow of each canoe.

"That must be Stu Osthoff's group," Gunnar said. "I wonder if they were planning to camp here. Hmm, probably not, since it's still so early. They're probably headed for Jean Creek and Burntside Lake."

Gunnar and Jack waved at the group and the group waved back but kept going. Gunnar recognized Stu paddling in the stern of the lead canoe.

"Stu — the guy in the lead canoe — is a top-notch fishing and canoe guide from Ely," he said. "We've been friends for a long time, though I've never been on a canoe trip with him. Anyway, tell me about your dad, Jack."

Jack looked down at his now-empty coffee cup. The mood was suddenly serious and Jack looked hesitant, as if he didn't know where to start.

"Sorry," he finally said. "I get emotional whenever I talk about my dad." He cleared his throat and took a deep breath. "I learned some time ago that the People's Army of Vietnam and the VC had stormed the command post where Dad was stationed in December 1970. I know a lot of Marines were killed, including my dad, but they managed to hold off the enemy.

"I was just a baby when he was killed, so I never knew him. My mom told me a lot of stories about him, how they met and fell in love and so forth. Dad graduated from Kansas University in Lawrence, Kansas, in May, 1969. He was in the Marine ROTC program. My folks got married in May 1969, before he went to Basic School.

He was deployed to Vietnam in December 1969 as a second lieutenant in charge of a platoon with the 1st Marine Division. He was meritoriously promoted to captain in February 1970. I was born in May, five months after he went to Vietnam."

"Your dad was a good man, Jack," Gunnar said quietly. "It had to be hard for him to leave your mom, knowing he was going to be a father. I remember him as a squared-away Marine. I was impressed with him from the first time I met him when I arrived in Da Nang in March 1970 and reported to him. He was my rifle company commander and he assigned me to take command of the first platoon. Everyone I talked to respected him as a leader who exemplified the motto 'Semper Fidelis.' He met with all the junior officers just after I arrived. Told us he was from Kansas, was married and that his wife was expecting their first child."

"Is there anything more you can remember about him?"

"I remember he wasn't as tall as me," Gunnar said with a chuckle. "But, then, not many people are — I'm about six-four. Still, your dad stood straight as an arrow and had a natural, commanding presence. He was soft-spoken and treated the men under his command with respect. I felt that Captain Riley would never ask his men to do something he himself wouldn't do, like ordering us into an encounter that was suicidal just to prove a point. He believed in the rule that a Marine leader's duty is to accomplish his mission *and* take care of his men. I don't remember if he talked any more about his family but he did have pictures of your mom and he showed them to me and some of the other officers. It was obvious your dad really missed your mom."

Jack sat there on the ground for a minute with his eyes closed. Finally, he looked up at Gunnar. "Thank you, Gunnar. I can't tell you how much I appreciate what you have told me. Do you have any regrets about having been in Vietnam and all you went through? Was it worth it?"

Gunnar thought about the question for a moment. "Jack, I'm proud to be a Marine and to have served in Vietnam," he finally said. "It was a senseless, political war, but really, aren't all wars politically motivated? War is such a horrible waste of life and money. A large gray slab of granite in Washington with the names of the 58,000 American military men and women who died in the Vietnam War stands as a reminder of that tragic time. Meanwhile, look at Vietnam. It's still a communist country. I think I remember reading somewhere that the U.S. imported more than $50 billion in manufactured goods from Vietnam last year, and it's a popular tourist stop in southeast Asia. Look at the aftermath of almost every war the U.S. has been involved in. We fight them and we kill each other and then we become friends. The losers are in graves around the world and the winners become golfing buddies. I'm not sure all is fair in love and war."

"I understand what you're saying," Jack said. "Unfortunately, it's a fact of life. I see it all the time in the workings of the government. Since we met last night, I've been thinking, too. As I was listening to you, I remembered one of the last letters Dad sent to Mom before he was killed. He mentioned one of his junior officers, Second Lieutenant Hansen, who had been seriously wounded while performing heroic actions that saved his platoon from being overrun. He said the tide of battle was reversed and the enemy withdrew, but not before many of them were killed. Dad said in his letter that he had recommended the office receive the Medal of Honor. Were you that officer, Gunnar?"

"Probably? I wasn't trying to be heroic," Gunnar said. "I was just trying to do my duty to protect my men and stop the enemy attack. I never took any pleasure in killing anyone when I was in Vietnam. Whenever I think about it now, I just feel sad. I was surprised to receive the Silver Star a year later. Such are the vagaries of war."

The two men shared a few more minutes of small talk as Jack prepared to head back to his camp. Emma's bark alerted them just as Bridgett approached.

"Sorry to break in on your meeting, guys," she said once she was within talking range. "Jack, what you think about moving on tomorrow rather than waiting until Wednesday? The Scouts are already getting restless. We could tackle the Maligne River and camp on Tanner Lake, have some time for fishing before moving on the next day to Darky Lake."

"I think that would be fine, Bridgett," Jack replied. "I guess this is goodbye for now, Gunnar. Where are you going from here?"

"Kind of back to where you guys came from," Gunnar explained. "I'm heading for Russell Lake and, eventually, south to Moose Lake and the canoe base. I'll call my son, Lucas, from there to pick me up and take me back to Duluth. By the way, Bridgett, my son Robert lives in Madison. Would you call him when you get back from this trip and let him know I'm okay?"

"Sure, Gunnar, I'll be happy to do that," Bridgett agreed. "Why don't we all trade phone numbers so we can keep in touch?"

"I was planning to ask for your number, Gunnar," Jack said. "I want to look at my dad's letter about the Medal of Honor when I get home. We'll touch base when we all get back from our trips."

It was midafternoon by the time Bridgett and Jack headed back to their camp. Gunnar was hungry, so he fixed some cheese and crackers, made another pot of coffee and decided to take a bath. He used to bathe in the lake but had discovered a better method. He filled his collapsible bucket about halfway with cold water then heated water in his 2-quart pot. Once the water was boiling, he poured it into the bucket. Standing behind his tent for privacy, he stripped off all of his clothes and poured some of the heated water from the bucket over himself. He lathered up with soap and rinsed the soap off with the rest of the water from the bucket. After drying off, he put on a clean T-shirt, skivvies and his canvas pants. While in camp, he also wore SAS lace-up, non-slip sneakers. Crocs and flip flops, in his opinion, were not safe because they didn't do well on wet surfaces. He had planned to do some bass fishing after his shower but was having quite a bit of groin pain and decided instead to take it easy. He was looking forward to fishing in Russell and Keats later in the week.

He fixed beef stew and butterscotch pudding for supper and boiled water for tea. He preferred Earl Grey, largely because it is flavored with oil of bergamot. After cleaning his dishes, he rested and watched the waxing moon setting in the west just after sunset. He had always been overwhelmed by the beauty of God's creation and looked forward to the end of the month, when the full moon would be visible. Even though he was tired, the amazing night sky full of stars held his attention until he finally gave up and he and Emma retired to their tent.

CHAPTER

14

Gunnar and Emma fell asleep listening to the sounds of the Scouts talking and singing in the camp across the point. When he started dreaming, it was about how happy he was to have survived his first deployment in Vietnam. He was sad to think about all his friends who were killed or wounded — a memory he didn't think he would ever forget — but the first thing he had done when he got back to Camp Pendleton on March 18, 1969, was to call his folks and then Kathleen.

"Kathleen, honey, is that you? I'm so glad to hear your voice. . . . Yes, I'm back in the States . . . at Camp Pendleton . . . I'm fine, just tired from jet lag. I talked to my folks . . . I'll be flying to Minneapolis on the 21st. Yes, they have the time of my arrival. I've really missed you, Kathleen . . . I love you, too. I'll be home for a month. Now, don't cry; I'll see you soon."

Gunnar's dream reminded him of how Kathleen had told him in one of her letters how she realized there had been something missing in her life until she met him. She also told him about the beginning discontent in America over the war. The thought of Gunnar being injured or killed was almost more than she could deal with. She prayed the rosary every day, asking the Blessed Mother to protect the man she loved. Then, one day in February she had received Gunnar's letter saying he would be returning to Camp Pendleton sometime in March and would call her.

It was 10 degrees below zero with a wind chill factor of minus 40 when Gunnar's plane landed at Minneapolis International on March 21, just before a major snow storm enveloped the Twin Cities. Gunnar's mom and dad — and Kathleen — were all there waiting for him.

"Hi, Mom; hi, Dad," Gunnar said as he spotted his family in the airport concourse, dropped his bag and swept his mom into a hug. After a moment in which neither of them seemed inclined to let go, Gunnar finally pulled back, if not entirely away. "I'm so happy to be home. I wasn't sure we were going to make it here with that storm coming in."

"We're glad you're home, too," his mom said, her voice cracking as she began to cry what Gunnar assumed were happy tears. "We worried about you all the time you were overseas."

Gunnar's dad looked like he might break down, too, but he didn't, just gripped Gunnar's shoulder for a long moment.

After a moment, Gunnar's mom dried her tears and stepped back enough to give Gunnar a once-over in his olive green "Service A" uniform.

"You look like you have lost some weight, dear," she said, a mix of concern and chastisement in her tone.

It was at that moment that Gunnar felt Kathleen's arms wrap around him and he turned away from his mother to kiss the crimson lips of the woman he loved. He could feel her tears falling, one landing on the side of his neck and soaking into the collar of his dress shirt. He didn't want to let her go, but he needed to catch his breath.

"I love you," he gasped. "I missed you."

"Me, too," she whispered. "I missed you so much."

When Kathleen and Gunnar finally became aware of their surroundings again, it was to see Gunnar's parents waiting patiently, a step away, having given the two lovebirds a moment of privacy amid the rush of the airport crowd.

"I'm really proud of you, Gunnar," his dad said. "I'm so happy you're home. Let's get your luggage and head to the hotel in St. Paul before the roads are shut down because of the snowstorm. Mom packed a suitcase of warm clothes for you, so you won't freeze to death in this Minnesota weather. I'll pull the station wagon up to the pickup area so we can get everyone loaded and you can change clothes before we head to St. Paul."

The trip from the airport to the hotel saw Gunnar and Kathleen seated together in the back seat, holding hands, with Gunnar's parents in the front.

"Your brother, Antonio, said he would meet us at the hotel," Gunnar's dad said, catching Gunnar's eye in the rear-view mirror. "But I'm not sure if he'll make it now with this storm. He's doing very well at the U, though he's in his third year and still isn't sure what he wants to do with himself. He likes math and physics, but that's as far as he's gotten on deciding a major."

"Let's pray that he makes it." Kathleen and Gunnar's mom spoke at the same time.

"Knowing Antonio, he will find a way to get to the hotel," Gunnar spoke up. "I hope so — I really want to see him. What about Anna and Sara? Are they going to be here?"

"Your sisters wanted to be here, but they had school and some things they had to do before you got home," his mom said, omitting the plans they were finalizing for Gunnar's welcome-home party. "They both send their love and are anxious to see you."

When Gunnar's parents had moved to Austin, before Gunnar was born, his father took a job working at Hormel, on what was called the "kill line." That was where they cut the throats of the hogs to drain the blood as the first step in the production of Spam. After working on the line for a few months, Gunnar's dad had shown his supervisors how they could make the process a lot more efficient and save money. He had always had a lot of moxie — a

Hansen family trait — and it was reflected in his work. It wasn't long before he started earning promotions — to the point where, by 1969, he was an executive at Hormel. As a result, he made a lot of business trips to the Twin Cities for meetings. Of course, Gunnar's mom frequently tagged along, and their favorite place to stay on those trips was the historic St. Paul Hotel in downtown St. Paul. They had made reservations to stay there again after meeting Gunnar at the airport.

Gunnar's folks had reserved an Ambassador Suite for themselves and a room each for Kathleen and Gunnar. The foursome finally made it to the hotel before the roads became impassable — the whole city was shut down by 8pm. They were happily surprised to find Antonio waiting in the lobby when they arrived.

"Antonio, it's great to see you," Gunnar said with a huge smile. "We weren't sure you would make it."

"One of my friends who lives in St. Paul gave me a lift on his Snowmobile," Antonio replied, his smile just as wide as he pulled his brother into a tight hug. "It's great to see you, Gunnar. I'm anxious to hear about Vietnam."

After getting checked in, the group decided to have a drink at the lobby bar before heading to their rooms to freshen up before dinner at the famous St. Paul Grill. After dinner, they all returned to Gunnar's parents' suite and talked for another hour or so before retiring to their own rooms — Antonio bunking with Gunnar — at the end of a long, full day. The plan had been to stay in St. Paul one night before heading home to Austin, but the weather meant they ended up staying two nights, with roads closed to travel. By the time they checked out, the cold front had moved to the east and the temperature had moderated. The drive to Austin, about 100 miles south of St. Paul still took a couple of hours. Gunnar was happy to see Anna and Sara, who were 17 and 16 at the time, and be home again. His welcome-home party was a true surprise and went off as planned, though Kathleen's folks couldn't make it because of the weather.

After spending a week in Austin, Gunnar drove Kathleen and Antonio back to Minneapolis. Kathleen had to get back to medical school and Antonio had interviews lined up for graduate school. Gunnar stayed with Antonio at his apartment and they spent some quality time catching up. They had always been very close and it felt good to have that time together. Of course, Gunnar also found time to see Kathleen almost every day. He had been so focused on trying to stay alive in Vietnam that he had almost forgotten how much he missed her — until he saw her waiting for him at the airport. When they kissed, it was like nothing Gunnar had experienced before, almost like their first kiss all over again, except somehow even better. Gunnar's pulse increased, he felt lightheaded and it truly felt as if there were butterflies in his stomach. He didn't want to let her go. The butterflies in his stomach only fluttered harder when she said she felt the same way. She had likened it to the same thrilling sensation she experienced when she was floating through the air after going down the ski jump in Ely.

"What are your plans now, my dear?" she asked. "Where do you think you might be stationed next?"

"I'll be going back to Camp Pendleton for now," he replied. "Before I left Vietnam, my CO asked me to consider applying for Officer Candidate School. I'm going to see if I can meet with my recruiter to find out more about it before I go back to California. If I do, I'll have to go back to 'Nam for a second tour, but it will be as a junior officer."

"Oh, Gunnar," Kathleen breathed out. "I don't want you to go back to Vietnam."

"I know, Kathleen," he tried to reassure her. "I'm not anxious to go back there again, either, but I feel I have a moral obligation to see this through, for my friends who already have made the ultimate sacrifice, or will before this is over." He brushed a thumb along her cheekbone, in a bid to soothe both of them. "Let's not talk about that now, though. It may never happen. Being here with you now is such a joy. It has helped me to almost forget about Vietnam. I'm starting to relax, and I've been thinking a lot about the summers we had together in Ely before I joined the Corps."

Gunnar took Kathleen's hands in his, looking down at where they were clasped between them. He hesitated, though there really was no reason. He had no doubts.

"I have an important question to ask you, Kathleen Andersson. Will you marry me?"

Kathleen's face broke into a smile, even as her eyes welled up with tears. "Yes, Gunnar Hansen," she said with certainty. "I will marry you."

Gunnar wrapped Kathleen in his arms then and kissed her. When they finally broke apart for air, they stayed within the circle of each other's arms.

"I know we can't get married right now," Gunnar finally said. "But I want you to wear my ring. Just as soon as I buy it."

"When we do get married, Gunnar, I want to do it in Ely, in July, have a big wedding reception, and go on a canoe trip for our honeymoon."

"So you've been thinking about it?" Gunnar teased fondly. "That all sounds good to me. I still have two weeks of leave. Why don't we drive up to Ely this weekend and tell your folks? That will give me time to find an engagement ring for you."

Kathleen thought that was a good idea and they left Minneapolis early Friday, April 4. It usually takes about five hours to drive the 260 miles to Ely, but it took them more than seven hours because the last 50 miles on Highway 169 from Virginia to Ely was snow-covered and hazardous.

Lucas and Mary Kathleen were overjoyed to see the two of

them. It didn't take Kathleen long to get to the point of why they were there.

"Mom and Dad, Gunnar and I got engaged and we wanted you to be the first to know. Isn't my ring beautiful? I'm so happy. I love Gunnar so much."

"Oh, Kathleen," her mom, Mary Kathleen, said. "That's wonderful news. We're so happy for you both. I know we don't have much time, but we have to celebrate this occasion. How about I call a few friends and we'll have an impromptu engagement party tomorrow afternoon?"

For a spur-of-the-moment gathering, everyone had a great time. Kathleen's sisters, Elsa and Agnes, who were attending Ely Junior College, were there, along with some friends and neighbors. Kathleen's dad, Lucas, took them out Saturday night for dinner after the party and, on Sunday morning, April 6, they had brunch at Vertine's after 10:30 a.m. Mass, during which Father Olson had given the young couple a special blessing. Gunnar was pleased to see Vertine's still had the homemade cinnamon buns that he loved so well, and he ordered a few extras to take with him when he and Kathleen headed back to Minneapolis.

15

Gunnar woke to the sound of thunder and rain sometime in the early morning hours of July 17, Day 7 of his trip. It was still dark outside. Everything was dry in the tent and he quickly went back to sleep. When he and Emma finally got up, the storm had broken, the sun was shining and Gunnar was hungry. After coffee, oatmeal with brown sugar and three slices of bacon, he felt much better. The sun quickly dried his tent and, within an hour, he was ready to move on to Russell Lake.

The wind was favorable as he paddled in a northeasterly direction toward Scripture Island, where he stopped for a break and some trail mix. He hadn't seen any other canoes since he had spotted Stu's group a day earlier. He thought how nice it was to have Emma in the bow to balance the canoe. Most of the time she fell asleep with the gentle rocking motion of the canoe. He turned southeast through the narrows and headed almost due east to the portage that ended on the west side of Russell in a small bay. The sky was hazy so the overhead sun wasn't as penetrating as it had been when he started the trip. It took him three trips to complete the 540-meter portage. He then continued due east in Russell for about 2 miles, to a nice campsite on a point. It faced northwest and was protected by a stand of large white and red pines. While it did provide some protection from the wind, he still had nice views of the sunset and sunrise.

As far as he could tell, it was midafternoon when he got to the campsite. After unloading his canoe, Gunnar carried it up a slight incline to where there was a small fireplace and some stacked firewood.

He was too tired to go fishing but he needed some nourishment since he hadn't had any lunch. He made a pot of coffee and ate some peanut butter and crackers. Emma had jumped in the lake when they landed and now she was drying off in the sun as she rested next to Gunnar. He gave her some doggie treats and put up his tent in a flat area covered with pine needles. The fragrance of the pines was quite pungent as the wind blew through them. "Wilderness perfume," as he called it, was one of the things he treasured about being in the Quetico. It was like a drug that stimulated his olfactory system and gave him a sense of tranquility, much like the haunting loon call at night and the occasional howling of the wolves that stimulated his auditory senses. His friend, Sig Olson, had written a wonderful book about it years ago, *The Singing Wilderness*. It was Gunnar's favorite book about the canoe country and it inspired him to write a poem based on Sig's book. He had memorized the words of the poem and thought about it now:

"Wilderness Symphony"

"He first heard it in the canoe country up north.
He listened to the music, my old
Friend, Sig Olson, as he set forth
On his many trips into the woods. He told
Us he could hear a symphony of sounds:
The wind rustling the branches of the pines
And water rushing along as it pounds
Against the shore in a storm. The sign
That all is well when the haunting trill
Of the loons cavorting in the lake

Remind us that we are home again and feel the thrill
Of being once more in our wilderness escape,
The singing wilderness.

How does one describe the symphony,
The music of the wilderness,
Wherever it may be? It's not a cacophony of sound.
It's more like a peaceful stillness.
Music that envelops one and soothes
Life's burdens, cares and woes.
It's the absence of noise, whose
Presence ruins the equanimity that flows
From the tranquility of the quiet sound
Of silence. Most of the world has never heard
This symphony of which we speak nor found
The peacefulness they seek nor heard the words,
Of 'the singing wilderness.'"

Freeze-dried chicken and dumplings, tapioca pudding and hot
tea was the first truly satisfying meal Gunnar had eaten since he
left home. His appetite hadn't been too good, probably a result of
the meds he was taking. The lemonade vodka concoction also was
enjoyable. He cooked supper on his Coleman stove and then stoked
up the fireplace to heat water for the dishes. It was still light by the
time he got everything cleaned up. He had planned to move on to
Keats Lake tomorrow but decided to stay another day in Russell to
rest and do some fishing.

One of the things he liked about Quetico Park was how there
were fewer people who camped there than in the BWCAW. There
were a couple of reasons for that. The camping fees were much
higher in Quetico and there were no pre-designated campsites. All
of the BWCAW campsites had a heavy steel grate on which you
were supposed to build your campfire and cook, and a fiberglass

biffy placed back in the woods away from the campsite. Ever since his first canoe trip when he was 16, Gunnar had preferred the Quetico. The portages were also less traveled and often more difficult.

The word *portage* comes from the French word "to carry." Gunnar was so used to portaging — carrying his packs and canoe from lake to lake on canoe trips — that he never thought much about it. Portages can be a real challenge, both physically and psychologically, especially for the uninitiated. Like it or not, portaging is an integral part of canoe trips in the boundary waters of the Quetico-Superior region. While portages can be a frustrating nuisance, Gunnar always had viewed them as an opportunity to take a break from paddling and enjoy the scenery along the trail. There also was the anticipation of the next lake at the end of the portage. Most of the portages he had taken so far on his trip had been pretty level and well maintained by the portage crews that kept the paths cleared of blockages from downed trees.

Thinking ahead about the rest of the trip, he remembered there were some coming up that might be more difficult, especially the one from Cairn to Sark and the ones from Kahshahpiwi to Joyce. The most difficult portage he had ever taken was years ago, when he was working at the canoe base. That was the 1,100-meter portage from Tanner Lake to Darky Creek. In addition to several downed trees blocking the trail, half of the trail was obscured by knee-deep — and, in some places, waist-deep — water. He had taken that portage the first time in 1962, when he was a swamper — a guide in training — with a crew from Sommers, and again in 1963, when he was guiding a crew of Scouts from Texas. Another difficult portage was the one from Yum Yum Lake to Kahshahpiwi. It's not necessarily the length of the portage that made it difficult. Rather it's how many boulders, downed trees, mud holes and hills that add to the challenge. Yum Yum had it all: a 1,200-meter-long walk over hilly terrain, and lots of rocks and mud holes.

16

July 18, Day 8 of his trip, was a perfect wilderness day. The temperature was in the 70s with a light breeze from the west and a cloudless, azure sky. It was too early to fish for walleye so he decided to do some exploring. Russell is a big lake with an irregular shoreline and a couple of big islands in the eastern part of the lake. The islands were too far away to explore that day. Instead, the little bay just to the west of his camp looked interesting, and there was a large beaver lodge near the south end of the bay where he could pick up some firewood. He sat in the front seat of the canoe, facing the stern, with Emma in the stern to balance things out. He attached a Rapala Vibrax Spinner lure to his fishing line and pushed off.

He paddled slowly toward the beaver lodge and spied a beaver in the water, heading for the lodge while dragging an aspen branch. He stopped paddling and drifted, hoping not to disturb the beaver. Emma had fallen asleep on the bottom of the canoe. Gunnar counted that as a good thing, since she would probably start barking if she saw the beaver. As the beaver got closer to the lodge, it suddenly dove under the water, pulling the branch with it. Gunnar waited for a few minutes, but the beaver didn't reappear. He was about 40 meters from the lodge, so he tried casting the Vibrax Spinner. He had an immediate strike and caught a medium smallmouth that he released. He caught and released a few more before deciding to move on to explore the rest of the shoreline. First, though, he loaded a few pieces of the gray, sun-dried beaver wood from the top of the lodge into his canoe. It would save him some work later.

Gunnar was in a good mood. The beautiful weather and the lack of pain that day helped, but it was more than that. He had come to the realization that he didn't need to be anxious about the future. He recalled what he had learned in his high school theology class with Brother Frank Clapp. It was one of his favorite passages in the Old Testament, Ecclesiastes 3:1-2:

> *For everything there is a season, and a time*
> *for every matter under heaven:*
> *a time to be born, and a time to die;*

He realized, maybe for the first time, that he wasn't in control of when or if the cancer would win the battle for his life. He just had to follow Dr. Lister's treatment plan and put his trust in God.

The rest he was getting on the trip was doing him good and his appetite was improving. He was happy he had stayed an extra day in Russell. Tomorrow's journey would take him to Keats Lake, where he also planned to stay two nights and do some serious fishing. He and Kathleen had enjoyed Keats each time they camped there in the past.

Gunnar was up just after sunrise on July 19, the ninth day of his trip. He felt rested and was eager to move on. It didn't take long to get everything packed. He made a pot of tea and munched on a hardtack biscuit as he was packing up. He had a 3-mile paddle across Russell and then a 410-meter uphill portage to Chatterton Lake. The prevailing wind out of the west helped to push him along; he and Emma were sitting at the end of the portage in Chatterton around noon, by his estimate. Lunch was a bowl of soup that he prepared on his propane stove, along with peanut butter crackers and a pack of chocolate and cashews trail mix. After resting for an hour or so, he paddled south in Chatterton to the 25-meter portage into McDougall Lake. A turtle was sunning on a log at the end of the portage but dropped into the water before Emma could get to it. Gunnar had to make three trips on the 350-meter portage into Keats, but he still felt pretty good after. About a half-mile south of the portage, there was a beautiful campsite on a point where he and Kathleen had camped years ago. It was unoccupied. He set up his tent on a flat area with a view of the lake and protected from the wind by a stand of trees. He stacked the remaining beaver wood from what he had picked at the last portage next to a small rock fireplace. Once things were organized, he assembled his rod and reel and attached a Rapala Shad Rap No. 7 to the line. Sitting on the front seat of his canoe, facing Emma in the stern, Gunnar paddled to a spot about 25 meters off the point and quickly landed two 17-inch walleyes for dinner. He put the fish guts on a rock away from the campsite for the gulls. Tomorrow he would set up his medium-heavy St. Croix rod with the Pflueger reel and 12-pound test line, hoping to hook a northern pike.

He enjoyed another beautiful sunset as he sat with Emma by the campfire. He could hear the constant sound of Split Rock Falls off to the north. Thoughts of Kathleen came to mind. She was sitting in front of the fire, trying to dry off after swimming in the cold waters of Keats and laughing at something he said. He covered her shoulders with a towel and held her close, kissed her wet lips. Something snapped his attention back to the present and the memory faded. He blinked and brushed tears from his eyes before patting Emma. He heated some water for tea before turning in for the night.

Sleep came quickly as images of giant fish swam through his dreams.

It was overcast when Gunnar awoke on Day 10, July 20. It looked like it might rain, so he rigged the rain tarp over the fireplace. Fishing was uppermost in his mind, in spite of the weather. He attached a Rapala Deep Diving Tail Dancer with a 12-inch titanium leader and swivel to the 12-pound test braided line. With Emma in the stern, he sat again in the canoe's front seat facing her. Since he was paddling solo, this maneuver provided more balance in the canoe when he was fishing. He zipped up his lifejacket and stowed his rain parka and fishing gear under the seat. He paddled slowly, trolling his lure, in a northeasterly direction. The fishing rod projected out on the port side of the canoe, secured between his legs. The line escaped from the reel quickly until he cranked the bail in place and set the drag. The lake was calm.

As he approached the small island just to the south of Split Rock Falls, there was a tug on his line. At first it felt like a snag, but back paddling didn't stop the tugging and, in fact, more line started to leave the reel. The drag started zinging as he adjusted it and he was able to reel in some line, only to have it peel out again. His rod was bending, the tip almost touching the water. Whatever was on the end of the line was slowly pulling the canoe back toward his camp. Emma sat up and watched him struggle, barking occasionally in encouragement.

Gunnar lost track of time as the battle continued. He gradually was able to reel in more line before it went slack and he realized the fish was coming up rather than going deeper. He started reeling in as fast as he could. The water suddenly exploded as the fish surfaced. Emma barked and Gunnar stared in amazement at the enormous northern pike resting next to the canoe.

"Look at that fish, Emma," he crowed "It must be at least 3-feet long!" Emma stood up in the canoe and barked at the fish. "Sit down!" he commanded. "I'll try to grab it."

That was a mistake.

As soon as he reached for the fish with his net, it dove under the canoe, almost taking the rod and reel with it and nearly swamping the canoe. Gunnar grabbed the rod at the last moment and held on for dear life. The drag started zinging again as the line rapidly left the spool. He finally was able to adjust the drag, which slowed things a bit, and the fish finally stopped running. It started raining, gently at first and then a steady downpour. He was too busy fighting the fish to worry about his rain parka. Emma gave Gunnar an encouraging bark and sat attentively, watching the drama unfold.

After what might have been an hour — Gunnar had lost track of time — the pike finally surfaced again, apparently defeated. As it swam next to the canoe, Gunnar carefully used his canoe paddle to try to estimate the length of the fish. It was awkward, but the fish cooperated long enough for him to get a good comparison. Gunnar was trying to decide how he could haul the fish into the canoe when the pike jumped up, spit out the Rapala and dove back into the water.

Gunnar couldn't believe it! His heart was racing and he was soaked with sweat and rain. He took a moment to catch his breath and comprehend everything that had just occurred. After a moment, he used the measuring tape in his tackle box to determine the length of the fish, which had extended from the tip of his paddle blade to the upper part of the paddle shaft, around 42 inches. While smaller than the muskies he used to fish for in Wisconsin — a 50-inch, 28-pound musky he had caught in Boulder Lake had been a real prize — this pike wasn't far off. Still trying to deal with all the excitement, he suddenly realized he needed to get back to camp and change into some dry clothes.

Back on dry land, Gunnar got a fire started and heated water for tea. The battle with the fish had physically drained him. His tachycardia had subsided, but he was still tired. He snacked on peanut butter and crackers and raisins before retiring with Emma to the tent for a nap.

Raindrops hitting the roof of the tent had a soothing effect as he drifted off to sleep; the rain had stopped when he finally woke up to a beautiful sunset. The fire had burned down and there was a chill in the air. He restarted the fire and sat on a log, warming himself. In spite of losing the pike, his sweet and sour pork freeze-dried dinner and some of the lemonade concoction satisfied his hunger and relaxed him. Mosquitoes were out after the rain, so he quickly got things cleaned up and stored the packs under his canoe before retreating with Emma into the tent. He opened his Bible, the same one that had seen him through his two deployments to Vietnam and the years of life since, and read his favorite passage in the New Testament from the first letter of Paul to the Corinthians: 1 Corinthians 13:1-13. He often wondered if that passage had been the inspiration for Shakespeare's Sonnet 110.*

After emptying his urine bag one more time for the night, he snuggled into his sleeping bag, Emma at his feet, and fell into a deep sleep.

---

* This number of Shakespeare's sonnet is from the new numbering system published by Sir Denys Bray in 1925 in his book, *The Original Order of Shakespeare's Sonnets*. The first line of # 110 is, "Let me not to the marriage of true minds." In the 1609 edition of Shakespeare's sonnets, #110 was listed as #116.

CHAPTER

17

Gunnar returned to Camp Pendleton from leave on April 21, 1969. It had been difficult to leave Kathleen, with whom he had shared the essence of his meeting with Staff Sergeant Jones.

"Gunnar, let me give you the straight scoop on Officer Candidate School," the staff sergeant had said. "I know you meet the college-graduate requirement. More important than a college degree, though, OCS candidates need physical and mental fitness. Scoring high on the physical fitness test, PFT, is very important. The best score you can get is 300. OCS is 10 weeks of training, after which you're commissioned as a second lieutenant. If you graduate, you go to Basic School at Quantico for six months."

"It sounds like a real challenge, Sergeant Jones," Gunnar had replied.

"It's difficult, Gunnar, but I know you can do it. You'll make a fine officer."

Gunnar graduated from OCS on August 9, 1969, and was commissioned a second lieutenant. He had one week of leave after graduation, so he met Kathleen and her sister, Elsa, in Washington, D.C. None of them had been to D.C. before, so they packed a lot of sightseeing in during the short time they had. A day trip down the Potomac River to Mount Vernon was their favorite. The week ended all too soon, with Gunnar saying goodbye to Kathleen and Elsa at Washington National Airport and heading back to Quantico for Basic School.

Basic School was a real challenge. The purpose of Basic School is to teach young officers what it means to be a Marine Officer and to develop the skill necessary to lead an infantry platoon. It's six months of tough training, and not everyone finishes.

OCS and Basic School were mentally and physically demanding. Gunnar finished Basic School in good shape and was happy it was over. His class graduated on February 14, 1970, and, as expected, Gunnar soon received orders to return to Vietnam as a platoon commander with the 1st Marine Division. His departure from San Diego was scheduled for February 28, so he took some leave to fly back to Minnesota for a few days to visit Kathleen and his parents. It was a good visit, however brief.

Gunnar arrived at Da Nang Air Base in Vietnam on March 3, 1970, as part of the 1st Marine Division. (It replaced the 3rd Marine Division, which had been redeployed to Okinawa in November 1969.) Gunnar reported to his rifle company commander, Captain Jack Riley, and was assigned to take command of the first platoon. The platoon consisted of three squads of 13 men each, divided into three fire teams and a team leader, usually a corporal. Sergeant Sam Boyd led the first squad and Sergeant Jeff Wilkins led the second squad. They had been in the country for six months and were experienced Marines. The third squad leader, Sergeant Ted Bolton, had been killed in action two weeks earlier and had not been replaced. Gunnar introduced himself to sergeants Boyd and Wilkins and told them that, even though he had served in Vietnam a year earlier with the 3rd Marines, he was relying on their experience to make sure they accomplished their mission.

Captain Riley had a meeting with all the junior officers, noting that Chu Lai would be the new headquarters of the 1st Marine Division. Chu Lai was about 55 miles southwest of Da Nang, on the coast of Vietnam. The plan was to concentrate the fight against the enemy in the southern provinces of Quang Tin and Quang Ngni, both south of Chu Lai, and that is where Gunnar was deployed until August. It had been the site of frequent incursions for some time, especially an area just to the west called Death Valley. It had more or less been kept under control throughout the war, but the enemy was never completely eliminated. Another problem that manifested itself early in 1970 was the inundation of South Vietnam with nearly pure cheap heroin from China, an apparent attempt to ensnare the American fighting forces. In late August 1970, the 1st Marine Division and portions of the 7th Marine Regiment began plans for a large operation to hopefully resolve the problem that was the Que Son District. Operation Imperial Lake was the last operation of the 1st Marine Division in Vietnam.

On September 3, after an initial 24 hours of artillery bombardment followed by air strikes, they were flown inland by choppers from the USS Okinawa, positioned about 10 miles off the coast of Vietnam in the Gulf of Tonkin. Captain Riley and Gunnar's platoon were the first units to be airlifted. The other platoons in Company E followed. Sergeants Boyd and Wilkins were, miraculously, still alive and in charge of their squads, and Staff Sergeant Chuck Smith was now leading the third squad. While everyone was waiting to board the choppers, Gunnar addressed his platoon:

"Marines, I want to make sure you understand the scope of our mission," he said. "We've been together for the past five months and I'm proud of all of your efforts. I don't know what scuttlebutt you've heard. The VC and the People's Army of Vietnam, as you know, have infected this area for years, in spite of our many attempts to eliminate them. Our new mission is to finally clean out the rat's nest and provide security for the command post. Do you have any questions?"

"Any idea, Sir, how long will we be here? And will our platoon take the lead?"

"I can't answer those questions," Gunnar said truthfully. "It will be up to the skipper as to who leads. And we'll take as long as is necessary to complete the mission. Now, let's get loaded on the choppers."

The command post was established on Hill 845 in Quang Nam Province. Recon patrols began scouting the area, but there was very little contact with the enemy. It was as if they had all been killed by the initial bombardment. Then the command post started receiving intermittent mortar fire, and there were reports of VC activity to the west and south. In spite of monsoons and heavy cloud cover, Captain Riley ordered two rifle platoons, Gunnar's platoon and the second platoon from Company E to form a wide perimeter about 200 meters from the command post, hoping to engage the enemy.

Being in the Que Son mountains was a challenge. One had to account for all the trees and underbrush, as well as the irregular topography. Gunnar cautioned his platoon to try to maintain some visual contact so, if one squad was hit hard, the other squads could provide support. Everyone carried M-16 rifles with 20-round magazines and there was one M60 machine gun team for each platoon. Each team consisted of four men: one man to shoot, one man to load and feed the ammo belts and two men to protect the team and carry the ammo belts. Everyone wore flak jackets, cartridge belts filled with ammo and grenades, and canteens of water.

By the time they had traveled about 100 meters from the command post, they were all sweating from the 100-degree heat and humidity. They stopped to rest before moving on another 75 meters. That's when they started receiving sniper and machine gun fire from a stand of tall trees surrounded by heavy underbrush, about 50 meters directly in front of their position. The enemy was uphill, which made the Marines easier targets. The Marines were able to find some protection behind a ridge, but they still were getting pounded by the VC, especially Sergeant Boyd's first squad.

"Sam, try to pull back," Gunnar yelled, though he wasn't sure his command could be heard over the noise of the guns and grenades.

Either way, the first squad didn't move. The amount of gun smoke in the air made it hard to see, and Gunnar radioed for air support. Captain Riley ordered everyone to fall back, but it was impossible. The Marines were returning the VC's fire but were receiving mortar salvos and heavy machine gun fire. Our machine gunners stayed busy returning fire, but they were either outgunned, outnumbered or both.

The second platoon had pushed 50 meters north of the first and wasn't being attacked like the first was.

Gunnar suddenly felt a sharp pain in his right thigh and realized he had been shot. There was a lot of blood on his uniform pant leg. He suspected the bullet had gone clear through the fleshy part of his thigh because he could still walk, though it hurt like hell. Corporal Simms, Gunnar's radio man, was next to him and Gunnar yelled for him to call for artillery. Simmse didn't respond. He had taken a hit to his chest and was crumpled on the ground, moaning. His radio was destroyed. Gunnar heard someone screaming at him and turned to see a Navy corpsman.

"Sir, sit down, and I'll tie a tourniquet around your thigh to try to stop the bleeding," he said. "Corporal Simms is dead."

The corpsman quickly applied the tourniquet, which did its job and stopped the bleeding. Then the corpsman was gone, on to his next patient. Gunnar thought he recognized the man in the moment but lost that mental image as all hell broke loose. There was still no air cover and Gunnar suspected his platoon was in deep shit. He yelled at Sergeants Wilkins and Smith to have their squads cover him.

"Simms is dead and our radio is kaput," he said. "I can't contact the Skipper to get his okay, but we need to do something ASAP."

Gunnar tried to explain briefly what he had in mind, though he wasn't sure how much the men heard with all the noise from the gunfire.

"I'm going to try to get behind the VC," he told them. "You keep pounding away at those bastards and pray the air support gets here soon."

With that, Gunnar grabbed his rifle and two cartridge belts full of ammo magazines and grenades. The second and third squads covered him as he made his way over to the first squad. Mortar shells kept falling but Gunnar kept moving, staying under cover as much as possible in a shallow ditch formed by a dried-up stream bed. The explosions continued unabated. The only sound Gunnar could hear was a loud ringing in his ears. He followed the stream bed south for about 30 meters. When he climbed out of the ditch, he saw that he was behind the copse of trees where the VC were dug in. He started throwing grenades at them and firing his rifle, which was on full automatic.

The VC started shooting at Gunnar but he kept up his attack. It wasn't much, but it was enough of a momentary distraction that it allowed the Marines from squads two and three to help the men in Squad one pull back to a safer position. Gunnar didn't recall much of the details, except that air support finally arrived — with 500-pound bombs and 20 mm rounds from their wing guns — and routed the enemy. Gunnar later learned that Sergeant Boyd had taken a lethal hit from a grenade.

Gunnar also had taken more fire before he had made it to safety, including a bullet to his left gut, just below his flak jacket. He had been able to keep moving and throw grenades after that one. He was starting to make his way back to his platoon when a bullet grazed the left side of his face along his jawline. That one knocked him out, though someone pulled him to safety. Gunnar was told later that one of their battlefield angels — as they sometimes called the Navy corpsmen, had saved his life. The man had been able to pack Gunnar's belly wound with hemostatic gauze and apply a large pressure dressing to tide him over until they could get him better medical care. Air evac choppers eventually arrived and transported Gunnar and the other wounded Marines to the USS Sanctuary hospital ship in the Gulf of Tonkin.

CHAPTER

18

Gunnar was up at sunrise the next morning, July 21, the eleventh day of his trip. He noticed a slight breeze from the west as he paddled across Keats on his way to Shelley Lake via Have-A-Smoke portage around Snake Falls. His goal for the day was Sark Lake, where there was a very nice campsite on the west side of the lake that he and Kathleen had shared years ago. As he started unloading his gear to begin the 300-meter portage, Emma barked. A moment later, a party of four young men appeared with their gear.

"Hello there," the fellow in the lead said. "How are you doing?"

"Good morning," Gunnar responded. "I'm doing fine, thank you. I'm Gunnar Hansen, and this is my dog, Emma. Don't worry, she won't bite you."

The men unloaded their two Kevlar canoes and their packs at the end of the portage away from Gunnar's gear.

"I'm Jim Daly," the fellow who had first spoken to Gunnar eventually said. "The guy with the Yankee cap is my brother, Ed. The other two are our fishing buddies, Jim Mertensotto and Joe Clark. This is our third canoe trip together and we're hoping the walleyes are biting."

"You should do okay in Keats," Gunnar reassured. "There's a great campsite directly across the lake that I just vacated. Speaking of, I should get going. I'm heading for Sark Lake tonight."

"Why don't you let us help carry your stuff over the portage?"

Jim asked. "We have to go back for a couple of things anyway."

"That's very kind of you, Jim," Gunnar said. "I appreciate your offer."

And with that, the four guys picked up Gunnar's canoe and packs, and Gunnar and Emma followed along behind them. He was impressed by their thoughtfulness.

"Thanks very much, fellows," he said as they arrived at the end of the portage. "You saved me a lot of time and work. It's much appreciated. Especially since it looks like it's starting to cloud over and we may be in for some rain. That always makes canoe travel more difficult."

Gunnar was happy to find the current wasn't too bad as he paddled through Shelley. Paddling against the current in Kahshahpiwi Creek was more of a struggle. He made sure to hug the western shoreline of the creek as he paddled past Kawnipi Forks, where he and Kathleen had swamped their canoe 20 years ago by being too close to the water pouring out of Kawnipi into the creek. The three portages along the creek to Carin Lake were all about 75-meters long and, aside from being wet and muddy in places, were relatively easy for him.

Gunnar figured it was early afternoon when he got to Carin, because he was hungry. The overcast sky meant he couldn't use the sun's position to confirm his estimate. He found a nice campsite on an island a short paddle from the end of the last portage and stopped there to fix lunch and rest before tackling the 470-meter portage into Sark. He was sweating from the warm temperature and the humidity, and it felt like it would start raining before long.

"Emma, come have some lunch and some doggie biscuits," he called to his dog. "You've been a good traveler. I'm happy I brought you with me on this trip"

Emma sat down next to Gunnar and ate her own meal as he ate his lunch. Gunnar was about to suggest that they take a nap when he was startled by a clap of thunder that seemed to be right next to him. The next moment, it started pouring rain and he rushed to get the lunch materials back in their pack. He grabbed his rain parka and put it on, even though he was already soaked. The wind was blowing and there were some white caps on the lake, so he ducked under a stand of trees and waited for the storm to pass. While he was waiting, Gunnar prayed. By the time he completed the rosary, the wind had abated and the lake was calm except for the sound of raindrops hitting the water. The sudden storm had morphed into an afternoon rainshower. That, he could handle. He loaded Emma and his packs into their canoe and started paddling the two miles to the portage.

That portage proved to be Gunnar's biggest challenge on the trip so far. Aside from being long and having very uneven terrain, the trail was slippery and riddled with scattered mud puddles. The temperature also had dropped at least 20 degrees, and he started to shiver with the chill. He also had to make four trips over the portage. He carried his canoe first, but it was a struggle. The second and third trips, with one pack and paddle each time, were more difficult for him, and he had to stop to rest frequently. The rain had tapered to a fine mist but he felt like he was reaching his limit. By the time he had finished his fourth carry-over with his personal pack and rod case, he literally fell on his side as he tried to unload the pack from his back.

"Lord, help me," he prayed aloud. He was too weak to stand up and his clothes were soaked. "Give me the strength to go on. I trust in you."

Emma sat next to him and the warmth of her body helped, though he felt nauseous and dizzy and may have blacked out. When he finally came to, the rain had stopped, the sky was clear and the last rays of the sun were fading on the horizon. With all the strength and determination he could muster, he struggled to his feet and rooted through his pack for some chocolate trail mix. When the sugar had done its job and he was feeling less like he might pass out again, Gunnar loaded his canoe and started paddling south. It was two miles through the narrow part of Sark to the main body of the lake, then a mile or so due west to the campsite where he planned to stay the night. He continued to be hit by rolling waves of nausea, and he had trouble keeping the canoe lined up. His groin also was aching and he had a headache. His arms and shoulders also were letting him know they'd had their fill of paddling. Emma kept watch over Gunnar and barked periodic encouragement as he struggled.

When he finally reached the main body of the lake, he became disoriented. Looking across the lake to the campsite on the west shore, there appeared to be a light from a flickering campfire. He was confused and didn't know what to do. He was tired, wet, cold, hungry, weak. He closed his eyes to try to fight off another round of nausea and slumped in the canoe, seeing nothing but the darkness behind his eyelids. He drew his paddle into the canoe and it clattered as it fell from his hands. Despite having stopped paddling, he thought he could feel the canoe continuing to drift, pushed along by a sudden breeze from behind.

The last thing he remembered before passing out for a second time that day was someone pulling his canoe ashore.

When Gunnar came to, it was dark. He was warm and dry, wearing dry skivvies and a sweatshirt and tucked into his sleeping bag in his tent. Emma was curled up next to him, sound asleep. Still, he was too exhausted to puzzle out how he had arrived there and he quickly fell back into a sound sleep. The next time he woke, it was light outside and Emma was gone. He heard someone moving around outside the tent as he sat up and took stock of his surroundings. When he peeked outside his tent, a woman was standing next to the campsite's fireplace, tending a fire.

"Good morning, Gunnar," she said, presumably hearing the

rustle of the tent flap as Gunnar moved to join her. "I hope you slept well. I've been waiting for you. Why don't you put on some pants and come sit down. I have a fresh pot of coffee and I'm making oatmeal."

Gunnar was confused — he thought it was understandable in the circumstances. He was definitely at the campsite he had been heading for — was it yesterday? — but didn't remember actually arriving there.

Lacking answers but trusting that Emma seemed to trust this stranger, Gunnar retreated to his tent long enough to dress properly and return to the fire.

"Thank you," he finally said as she handed him a cup of coffee. "Yes, I slept well. I think. I'm . . . not quite sure what's going on. Who are you? And how did I get here?"

"I'm sorry, I didn't introduce myself," the woman apologized. "I'm Abigail Fraser. Your canoe washed up on the beach over there about 11 o'clock last night. You were delirious, drenched and shivering like crazy. Your dog was with you and your pack sacks were wet, lying on the floor of your canoe."

"Did I talk to you?" Gunnar asked. "I don't remember much of anything after I left the portage and started paddling this direction. This is where I had planned to camp. But that long portage and the rain did me in."

"That's understandable." Abigail nodded. "I'm just glad I was here to get you safely ashore."

"Me, too," Gunnar agreed, cupping his hands around the mug and taking a sip of coffee. Its warmth was like heaven. "Thank you. For the coffee and the rescue. I'm sorry you found me in such a state, though. I really am a good canoeist. Been doing it all my life. I've done pretty well so far. I didn't really realize just how bad it might get."

"That's understandable," Abigail agreed. "Especially when

you've been doing it for so long and know what you're usually capable of. When did you start your canoe trip, Gunnar?"

"On July 11th. I wasn't sure last night if I was going to make it any farther. How did you get me into my tent?"

"I pulled your canoe up on the beach — with you in it — and unloaded all your gear. Then I managed to get you out of the canoe and over here to the fireplace. You were pretty much out of it, but I got you to drink a cup of tea and eat some cookies."

"I do like tea and cookies," Gunnar said, his smile small and wry as he tried to lighten the mood. Dying in a canoe in the middle of the Quetico wouldn't be the worst way to go, but Gunnar was relieved that it hadn't happened the night before. And, if he were being honest, a bit shaken by how close he came.

"They're good cookies," Abigail played along. "Anyway, once you seemed a bit more together, I looked through your gear — sorry about that — and set up your tent. Your foam mat and sleeping bag were still dry, so I put those in your tent. Some of the clothes in your pack were wet. You still had a dry pair of skivvies and jeans but your sweatshirt was wet. The one you're wearing is one of mine. I also hung up most of your wet clothes on the line back there to dry."

"Thank you again." Gunnar was overwhelmed by the amount of trouble to which Abigail had gone to help him. Sure, that's what canoeists did in the wilderness. You find someone in need, you help.

"Oh, before tucking you in, I also drained that urine bag on your leg.

"I'm sorry you had to deal with that, too," Gunnar replied. "But I appreciate that you did."

"Not a problem," Abigail waved off his apology. "You have a very nice dog. I could tell she was worried about you last night. I think she's running around right now with my dog, Lizzie, who is also an English Springer Spaniel."

"Aren't they the best?" Gunnar's smile at the mention of the dogs was genuine and spread across his face. "Her name's Emma. It's good for her to have some company, and some exercise. She's been so patient, sitting in the canoe every day." He took another sip of his coffee. He was nearly finished and already debating whether he wanted another cup. "Wait . . . how do you know my name?"

"I found your Quetico travel permit with your name on it when I was getting the clothes out of your pack," Abigail replied. "I was expecting you earlier but the rain disrupted things. I'm sorry you got soaked and chilled before you got here. I think you will be fine for the rest of your trip, though."

Gunnar pondered her words for a moment before excusing himself and returning to his tent. Her words were confusing — what did she mean about expecting him earlier? — but . . . maybe he'd just misheard her. There also was something about Abigail that was familiar. When he tried to place her, though, his mind went to the Navy corpsman who had saved his life — not once but three times — in Vietnam. Maybe he was just linking the two because she, too, had saved his life. Still, he resolved to ask her before they parted ways if she had any relatives who had served in Vietnam.

19

On September 14, 1970, Gunnar's family in Austin received a telegram from the office of Captain Daniel R. Kelly, USN, Base Chaplain, Camp Pendleton Marine Corps Base, Oceanside, California.

The doorbell rang and Marie Hansen opened the door to find one of the neighborhood boys waiting.

"Hello, Billy, what are you doing here?" she asked.

"Hi, Mrs. Hansen," the 16-year-old replied, pointing at the logo on the hat he was wearing. "I'm working part time at Western Union and I have a telegram for you. My boss said it was important and he wanted it delivered in person."

"Well, thank you, Billy. Say hello to your boss and thank him."

She took the telegram and closed the door. The message was quite long and she read it slowly:

> *"Dear Mr. and Mrs. Hansen: Your son, 2nd Lieutenant Gunnar Charles Hansen, was wounded while on a combat mission in Vietnam on September 7, 1970, and is presently recovering on the hospital ship USS Sanctuary, off the coast of Vietnam. His injuries are such that he will not be able to return to combat. As soon as his condition is stable, he will be transferred to a Naval Medical Center for further treatment. You will be notified when he is transferred. If you have any questions, please contact*

*the base chaplain's office at Camp Pendleton, California,
phone number 713-336-7064.*

Sincerely, Captain Daniel R. Kelly, Chaplain, USN."

Marie started crying as she read the message and had to sit down.

Gunnar's sister Anne heard her and rushed to her side.

"What's wrong, Mom?"

"Gunnar's been killed in Vietnam," Marie said, handing her daughter the telegram. Anne quickly scanned the message.

"Mom," she said. "Gunnar hasn't been killed . . . he's been wounded, yes, but he's being treated. On a hospital ship. You just misread the message."

"Are you sure?" Marie asked as Anne handed the paper back to her to reread. "Oh, Anne, thank God. I just panicked. I worry about him over there all the time."

"It's okay, Mom." Anne hugged her reassuringly. "I'm going to call Dad and ask him to come home from work. He needs to be here. Maybe he can call and get some more information. I'll call and let Kathleen know, too."

Gunnar's dad, Charlie, arrived home not long after Anne reached him at his office and he spent a few minutes comforting Marie. The telegram was vague about the nature of Gunnar's injuries. On one hand, he was alive. On the other, he was hurt badly enough that they weren't going to send him back into combat. Charlie decided to call Captain Kelly to see what more he could find out. It was 10:30 a.m. Central Time when he placed the call.

"Camp Pendleton Marine Corps Base, chaplain's office. This is Corporal Jackson; how may I help you?"

"Hi, this is Charlie Hansen from Austin, Minnesota. I'm trying to reach Captain Kelly regarding a telegram I received today about my son, Second Lieutenant Gunnar Charles Hansen."

"Captain Kelly is not here at the present time, Sir. He's visiting patients at the base hospital, but he should be back in the office by 11 a.m. Pacific Time — 1 p.m. Central. Please give me your number and I'll ask him to return your call."

Charlie gave the corporal his phone number and thanked him before hanging up. It was about 5 p.m. before Captain Kelly finally called back. Even so, the best he could do was confirm what they knew from the telegram and promise to call them the next day, after he had talked to someone aboard the USS Sanctuary.

True to his word, Captain Kelly called back the next day.

"I was able to communicate with the information officer on the ship," he told Charlie. "He didn't have any news about your son's injuries other than that he is stable and awake. They plan to transfer him by chopper to Da Nang tomorrow, the 16th, and then he'll be loaded on a transport plane to Miramar Naval Air Station north of San Diego. He should arrive there about September 19th after the transport makes a stop in Okinawa. He'll be taken by ambulance to the U.S. Naval Hospital in San Diego. I will call you when he arrives in San Diego."

CHAPTER

20

Gunnar sat down on a log in front of the fireplace. He was hungry and consumed two bowls of oatmeal and raisins along with his coffee. He was still unsure how he managed to end up in this campsite, given his disorientation the night before.

"You look like you're not fully awake yet, Gunnar," Abigail said.

"Yes," Gunnar agreed. "I'm still a bit bewildered."

"It's okay. I know this whole situation must seem strange to you. I believe, sometimes, things happen that we can't explain. I'm just happy you're here, and safe and sound."

"It's fortunate you were here, Abigail," Gunnar said. "I can't thank you enough for saving me and taking care of me." He looked down at his bowl, which was again empty. "And for making such good oatmeal. This sure hit the spot. I didn't realize how hungry I was. If there's enough to spare, I'm going to have another cup of coffee."

"Help yourself."

The sun's warmth felt good as they cleaned their dishes. It was July 22, and he had made it to the twelfth day of his trip. "I wanted to mention I'm taking medication which has affected my strength. I think that is why I had such a difficult time on that last portage."

"What about you, Abigail?" he broke the easy silence as they finished up their tidying and settled back in at the fire. "You have to be pretty tough to take a canoe trip, much less a solo trip, man or woman. But it's clear you know your stuff — I really like that Souris River solo canoe of yours."

"Thanks for saying that, Gunnar," Abigail smiled. "I don't consider myself particularly tough, but I feel very confident that I can handle myself here in the wilderness. I'm originally from Toronto but I live in Duluth now. My husband, Bill, died of a heart attack six years ago. We lived in Thunder Bay when we first got married and we took our kids on a lot of Quetico trips. It was a great experience for all of us."

Just then, Emma and Lizzie ran up to where Gunnar and Abigail were seated.

"Good morning, girl," Gunnar greeted Emma with a ruffle of her ears. "I bet you're looking for breakfast." He looked at Abigail. "I can't believe I forgot to feed Emma. And that she let me."

"Don't worry, Gunnar," Abigail reassured him. "I fed both of them this morning, while you were still sleeping."

Abigail stood up to stretch. She was an attractive woman, Gunnar acknowledged to himself. She reminded him of Bridgett Olson, the woman he'd met back on Sturgeon Lake, except Abigail wore her brown hair fixed in a bun, like the women Marines used to do when he was in the service. She was a few inches shorter than Gunnar and looked to be in her forties, though he couldn't tell for sure. Her tanned, wrinkle-free face was perfectly proportioned. He still couldn't help thinking about how much she looked like the corpsman from Vietnam, though he hesitated to bring it up.

"I'm going to straighten up my tent and wash a few clothes," Abigail said. "I think your things are just about dry. Maybe we can continue our conversation later."

"That sounds like a good plan, Abigail," Gunnar agreed. "I need to check my stuff, too, and I want to change these jeans for my canvas pants."

Aside from his wet clothes, which were just about dry, the rest of Gunnar's gear survived the rainstorm unscathed. He was sitting on the sandy beach looking at the lake and enjoying the warmth of the sun when Abigail sat down next to him. She was wearing shorts, a bright yellow, long-sleeve knit shirt and tennis shoes.

"You never did finish telling me about yourself, Abigail," Gunnar hinted.

"Oh, there really isn't much to tell," she laughed. "I moved from Toronto to Thunder Bay, where I got a job at Lakehead University, teaching English literature. That was my major in graduate school. My husband, Bill, was a junior executive at the Lyric Paper Mill there. About 10 years ago, he was offered a position at the Newton mill in Cloquet, Minnesota, so we moved there and eventually became U.S. citizens. We have two children, Robert and Amanda. Anyway, when he died suddenly six years ago, I sold our home in Cloquet and moved to Duluth, where my daughter lives. My son moved back to Thunder Bay. I bought my Souris River solo canoe in Atikokan and started taking solo canoe trips three years ago. It's been very therapeutic for me, and Lizzie is a great companion."

"Have your solo trips all been in the Quetico?"

"Yes, but I didn't travel too far from Pickerel Lake on my first two trips. Robert stored my canoe at his place in Thunder Bay. I decided to venture further on this trip. I'm heading south, to Moose Lake in the BWCAW. My daughter, Amanda, drove me to Robert's place in Thunder Bay and he dropped me off at Stanton Bay, on the north side of Pickerel, on July 11. I arrived in Sark on July 20, the day before yesterday."

"Wow, that's quite a story," Gunnar enthused. "What do you do when you're not canoeing?"

"I try to keep active. I work out a couple of times a week at the Y and jog along the lakefront. I also do volunteer work at St.

Benedict's and play bridge once a week with a group of ladies from the hospital. Plus, I check on my grandchildren, so I keep busy."

"Did you ever think about going back to teaching, either at U of M Duluth or the College of St. Scholastica?"

"That's an interesting question," Abigail said, growing thought-ful. "Do you have any idea how colleges and universities have changed in terms of the liberal environment that exists on many campuses today? When I looked into the English departments at UMD and St. Scholastica, I was dismayed by the emphasis on equity, diversity and inclusivity, especially at St. Scholastica. Their Literature Department teaches Shakespeare, my specialty, from that perspective. I was turned off by their approach. The students are being brainwashed. I'm not sure about UMD but I couldn't deal with that philosophy."

"I fully understand what you're saying. I've read a lot about the problem. When my daughter, Marie, was in graduate school, she had to compete with students who were contaminated by the EDI philosophy and professors who subverted 'truth' to fit their secular liberal philosophy. It's a serious problem."

"It is," Abigail said.

"So, what are your plans now?" Gunnar asked. "Are you stay-ing here in Sark or moving on?"

"I'm headed for Moose Lake, where my daughter will meet me and drive me back to Duluth. I'm supposed to pick up a boat ride at Prairie Portage to take me to La Tourell's resort. What about you?"

"My plan is to leave Sark tomorrow and head for Joyce Lake," he said. "Eventually, I also plan to end up in Moose Lake, on or about August 1st. Since we're both headed for the same place, what do you think about traveling together? It would be nice to have some company on the rest of my trip. I've decided I'm not a great fan of solo canoe trips, not after what happened yesterday."

"You know, Gunnar, I agree with you about solo trips," Abigail replied. "I enjoy being alone for one or two days, but there is a point where too much loneliness isn't good for the soul. We're basically social creatures. So, yes, I think it would be fun to travel together."

That settled, Abigail checked her watch and realized it was already 3pm. They had been talking for almost four hours. She fixed a late lunch of chicken soup and lemonade. By the time they had finished eating and Abigail checked the clothesline, everything was dry.

"It's still early," she said. "Maybe we should discuss how we'll handle things for the rest of the trip. I'm curious about the route you plan to follow. Should we combine our food packs? You know, things like that."

"That's a good idea," Gunnar said. "Let me get my map out and I'll show you the route I want to follow." He disappeared into his tent, only to return to the fireplace a few minutes later. "The main purpose of my canoe trip is to visit some of the lakes and campsites that my wife, Kathleen, and I shared before her death. For example, we spent our honeymoon at a beautiful campsite on McIntyre Lake. Here, take a look at the map. From Sark I had planned to go to Joyce Lake. Then Conmee, McIntyre, Sarah and North Bay in Basswood and, finally, to Moose Lake."

"It looks like the two portages into Joyce are pretty long," Abigail said. "Do you think you can handle them?"

"If you had asked me that question last night, my answer would have been no. If you're going to be with me, though, I feel sure that I can handle them. I've been over those portages many times in the past. They're not unfamiliar. Just different circumstances this time. As far as our food packs, since most of our stuff is freeze-dried, let's put dinner rations in one pack and breakfast and lunch rations in the other pack. Whatever we do we'll keep the weight in each pack about the same and make it easier to find things."

In the course of rearranging their food packs, they decided

what to have for dinner and prepared it once they were done, eating in companionable silence. The mosquitoes were out in force after dinner. Gunnar and Abigail again cleaned their dishes and Gunnar showed Abigail his system for putting the packs under the canoe for safekeeping. Despite their lack of travel, it had been a full day and both were sleepy, so they retired to their tents. Gunnar fell asleep listening to the night sounds, Emma in her usual place at the foot of his sleeping bag. Even though she was a good companion, Gunnar realized he had been lonely for human companionship, someone with whom he could share his feelings. Someone like Abigail.

They were both up early the next morning, July 23, the thirteenth day of Gunnar's trip. After finishing their coffee and farina, it didn't take long to get packed. The first portage out of Sark to Keefer Lake was about 400 meters. The trail was muddy from the recent rain. It was next to a high rock formation on the west side of the trail. It took about two hours to complete the portage and another two hours for them to paddle the 3 miles across Keefer against a gentle headwind to the short portage into Kahshahpiwi. Gunnar told Abigail the first part of the long portage out of Kahshahpiwi was uphill. Then it leveled off and was pretty easy going the rest of the way, except for a few places along the trail where some soft ground was covered by wooden planks and rocks, if he recalled correctly.

Gunnar helped Abigail as they unloaded at the beginning of the 920-meter portage.

"Let's have a snack before we start," he said. "Why don't you make some peanut butter crackers and I'll make some lemonade. Then we can have lunch at the end of the portage when we get all the gear over."

"Sounds like a plan, Gunnar. I am hungry."

They did the portage in stages, like the French Voyageurs. It took them three trips over three hours. After a lunch of soup and trail mix at the end of the portage, they paddled across a small unnamed pothole to the 590-meter portage to Joyce Lake, refreshed and ready. It was late afternoon when they finally made it to Joyce. They were both anxious to get to the campsite, which was on a point about a mile from the portage.

"This is a beautiful campsite, Gunnar," Abigail said. "Have you been here before?"

"Kathleen and I camped here three or four times over the years," he acknowledged. "She really liked it, especially the sandy beach and view of the lake."

Emma and Lizzie explored the area while Gunnar set up his tent and Abigail got a fire started. He placed Abigail's canoe near the fireplace to use as a cooking table and placed his canoe by his tent. She set up her A-frame tent next to his while he boiled water for a freeze-dried chicken and dumplings dinner. He also made chocolate pudding for dessert and mixed a batch of lemonade and vodka. They relaxed on a large log as they ate their dinner.

"Abigail, are you familiar with the 'Wilderness Grace' that's recited before meals on a canoe trip?"

"I've never heard about it," she admitted. "Can you enlighten me? Where did you learn about it?"

"We said this all the time when I worked at the canoe base. I'll recite it for you:

"For food, for raiment, for life and opportunity,
for friendship and fellowship,
for sun and rain, for water and portage trails,
we thank thee Oh Lord, Amen."

"That's a beautiful prayer, Gunnar," Abigail said. "I need to write it down in my journal so I can memorize it."

She reached into one of her packs and pulled out a maybe 6-inch by 8-inch brown leather-bound book. The end of a green ribbon protruded from the bottom. She let Gunnar see the cover but didn't offer to show him the notes inside.

"I like to make notes about my canoe trips," she said. "It's interesting to look back at the comments I've made during the trip. It's like a diary. I try to write something before starting the trip and then each day of the trip."

"I think it's a good idea, if you are disciplined enough to do it," Gunnar agreed. "My daughter, Agnes, is the note keeper in our family. My record-keeping efforts haven't been too successful."

"You mentioned that you used to be a canoe guide at Sommers Canoe Base. What was that like?"

"Sommers is run by the Boy Scouts," Gunnar said. "I worked there as a canoe guide for three summers when I was in college. It was a great experience. I met a lot of neat people during that time, including my friend, Joe Seliga — you may have heard of him; he's from Ely and pretty well-known as a wooden canoe builder. Most importantly, that's when I met Kathleen — my wife — who also lived in Ely. I also did some commercial guiding for a couple of years before I joined the Marine Corps. I have many wonderful memories of that time."

Gunnar and Abigail listened to the loons calling as dusk settled in. He put more wood on the fire and heated water for tea to go with their pudding. She turned down his offer of Earl Grey in favor of her favorite, Chamomile. After they washed the dishes, they placed the food packs under her canoe and the dishes on the bottom to dry. Then they sat on the log, quietly watching the fire burn, the flames dancing in the breeze and moving back and forth like a child on a swing.

Gunner looked at Abigail and said, "This is my favorite time of the day, a time of peace and contemplation, when darkness envelops the world and the day is done."

CHAPTER

21

The choppers arrived and transported Gunnar and some of the other wounded Marines to the USS Sanctuary hospital ship late on the afternoon of September 7, 1970. The battle was over and the enemy had been defeated, at least for the time being. As they loaded Gunnar onto the chopper, he was awake but disoriented, at least in part a result of the morphine he was on for the pain. Blood covered the front of his uniform. When he was unloaded on the ship, a corpsman spoke to him first thing.

"Lieutenant Hansen, sir, you're bleeding quite a bit from a gut wound," the corpsman explained. "You'll be going to surgery ASAP."

Then he slapped a big bandage over the bleeding area on Gunnar's belly and applied pressure before wheeling him into the operating room. People wearing what looked to Gunnar to be green pajamas and masks surrounded him, all talking at once. He tried to tell them he couldn't hear in his left ear, but he had trouble opening his mouth because of what felt like the worst toothache ever in his left jaw. Somebody covered his mouth and nose with a mask — different from the ones worn by the people in green pajamas — and he could smell something sweet. He had the fleeting thought that it was gas.

Gunnar woke up in the recovery room.

The pain was bad. It seemed to be everywhere, especially his belly, and he was so dizzy he couldn't sit up. Waves of nausea accompanied the pain and dizziness. Gunnar felt like shit and wondered if he would have been better off dead.

They gave Gunnar morphine for the pain and Inapsine for the nausea; the only thing that helped his dizziness was Valium. Every time he tried to open his mouth, pain shot up to his deaf left ear and the side of his head. Gunnar's right thigh was swollen and wrapped in a bandage and whenever he tried to move it . . . pain, pain, pain. It took him a moment, but Gunnar eventually remembered that his thigh is where he had been shot first. His radioman, Corporal Simms, had been standing next to him and had been killed. He was a good Marine, Gunnar thought, tearing up. Gunnar was taken back to surgery the next day to have the packing in his belly wound changed. Medication in his IV fluid put him to sleep for the few minutes it took to do the procedure. Later that day, one of the doctors talked to Gunnar about his situation.

His name was Lieutenant Commander Sobol. He told Gunnar he had been in surgery for four hours after he first arrived on the ship. He had lost a lot of blood — replenished by a transfusion of 6 pints of blood plus salt water fluids — and had come close to dying. Once they had stopped the bleeding in Gunnar's gut, they realized the bullet had destroyed the lower end of his large bowel, the sigmoid, and also had injured his bladder. A left jaw fracture explained the pain of opening his mouth, caused by the same bullet that had knocked out the hearing in his left ear and probably affected the part of his ear that controlled my balance, which explained why he was so dizzy. The gunshot Gunnar had taken in his thigh, as painful as it was, was just a flesh wound and had not broken any bones.

"You're lucky to be alive, Lieutenant," the doctor said. "If that corpsman hadn't been able to stop the bleeding from your wounds

on the battlefield, you wouldn't have made it. You must have a powerful guardian angel. You were pretty well shot up, but here you
are, still alive."

Gunnar tried to reply but merely winced when he tried to open
his mouth to speak. The doctor waved him off.

"Right now, we're concerned about infection so you're getting
a lot of antibiotics," he continued. "You are going to need to have
more surgery in a few days to fix your fractured jaw, but you'll have
to wait until you get back to the States to have someone check your
ear. We did take some x-rays that showed your pelvis is fractured
on the left side, which also adds to your pain.

Gunnar tried to follow everything the doctor had told him about
his condition, but the haze from the medications he was on wasn't
helping. Instead, he clung to the general impression that he was
lucky to be there, lucky to be alive, and that he was going home.

A couple of days later, on September 10, a nurse told Gunnar they were planning to fix his jaw fracture later that day and
change the dressing on his belly wound. She helped him slide
out of his hospital bed into a chair. He got so dizzy he thought
he was going to fall.

"I know it's difficult for you to get up, but it's very important so
you don't get a blood clot in your lungs," the nurse said. "You need
to cough and do a lot of deep breathing."

"What's that long incision on my belly and those tubes sticking
out from it? And how long do I have to keep this tube in my penis?
It's not painful, but it's not comfortable, either."

"That incision is where the doctors had to open you up to remove
the damaged bowel," the nurse explained. "They also had to take
the end of the bowel and sew it to your skin so the bowel will drain
properly. That's called a colostomy. The tube in your penis is a catheter and the end is in your bladder. The bullet damaged the struc-
ture that drains fluid from your kidney. They were able to fix that,

but the catheter is there as a precaution to make sure the bladder heals okay."

The following day, Gunnar was surprised to have Captain Riley and Sergeants Wilkins and Smith visit. Captain Riley asked how Gunnar was doing before saying, if Gunnar felt up to it, he wanted to ask him some questions about the actions he had taken against the VC. Gunnar apologized for not contacting him to await orders but noted their radio had died along with Corporal Simms. The situation as Gunnar had seen it was desperate. His men were being slaughtered, the air support hadn't arrived and they couldn't call for artillery. Gunnar explained how he figured, if he could get behind the VC and pepper them with grenades and rifle fire, it would distract them long enough for the second and third squads to relieve the first squad, which was taking the brunt of the attack. The hope was it would hold off the VC long enough for the air support to arrive.

"When I got shot in my thigh and I saw Simms next to me, dying, something clicked in my brain," Gunnar explained. "I decided I wasn't going to let those sons of bitches wipe us out. I don't remember much after that, except I was determined to kill as many of them as possible so I could save my men.

"I guess you could say I had a feeling of rage. It was a feeling I've never had before. It's kind of frightening to think about that now." Gunnar paused in his retelling, trying to tamp down a sudden bout of nausea. "I'm sorry, Skipper, I'm not feeling well. I think I'm going to throw up."

Just then, the nurse walked in the room and Gunnar was true to his word. The nurse and a corpsman ran a tube through his nose into his stomach. It hurt when they inserted it, but that didn't keep Gunnar from continuing to throw up. They hooked the tube up to a suction machine and, before long, the vomiting stopped. They said my bowel hadn't started working properly since the surgery and, instead of his body's waste being expelled through the colostomy, everything was backing up. The nurse told Gunnar he had an ileus where the bowel doesn't contract normally after surgery.

It was another three days before the tube was finally removed.

Captain Riley had left the room when Gunnar got sick and was being tended to by the nurse and corpsman, but he left a note with Dr. Sobol, thanking Gunnar. He said he wanted Gunnar to know his actions had stopped the VC attack and saved a lot of lives before air support arrived. He promised to look up Gunnar after his tour ended in January 1971 and he returned to the States.

Gunnar continued to show slow but steady improvement and Dr. Sobol finally scheduled him to be transferred to San Diego, to the U.S. Naval Hospital at Balboa Park, on September 16. His information officer had already contacted the base chaplain at Camp Pendleton, who would contact his folks. Just before he left, one of the corpsmen removed the catheter. After a brief layover in Okinawa, a plane of wounded Marines — including Gunnar — landed at Miramar Naval Air Station on September 19. From there, they were taken by ambulance to Balboa. It was good to be home.

Gunnar's parents and fiancee arrived in San Diego on September 20 and visited Gunnar each day for the next week before they had to return to Minnesota and Kathleen had to go back to school. Gunnar was still in a lot of pain but didn't talk too much to his family about his wounds or how it all happened. His mom cried a lot at first, but his mom seemed reassured when Gunnar told them the doctors were optimistic he'd have a full recovery — except for the hearing loss in his left ear.

Kathleen and Gunnar held hands a lot, and Gunnar was convinced that having his family with him during that week really helped to hasten his recovery. He realized his family loved him and needed him, and he was determined to get well — not just for himself but for them, too.

Within a week of arriving in San Diego, Gunnar started on physical therapy. Even though his dizziness was better, he still couldn't walk unassisted. He not only felt generally lightheaded but, worse, had the sensation that everything was spinning around. The doctors had called it vertigo. Gradually, he was able to sit in a wheelchair and do leg exercises. X-rays of his jaw showed the metal plate that had been used to stabilize the fracture. Gunnar was having trouble getting his teeth to line up properly, so the surgeon put temporary braces on both his upper and lower teeth. The braces had little hooks on them to which he attached rubber bands to pull the teeth into proper position. The nurses worked with Gunnar to show him how to care for the colostomy resulting from the removal of his damaged sigmoid. He wasn't sure how he was going to live with that for the rest of his life.

Gunnar was taken back to surgery on October 6 to evaluate his bladder reconstruction. The ureter, the tube that drains urine into the bladder, was healing okay. The packing in his abdominal wound was removed and the drains were taken out. A week later, on October 13, an ear surgeon operated on his left ear. There wasn't much that could be done other than to clean up the wound to prevent infection. Gunnar's hearing in that ear was gone and the bullet also had knocked out the part of the ear that dealt with balance. That explained his dizziness. There also was a constant ringing in his left ear. Gunnar was transferred to the hospital's rehab unit on October 20. He was now able to walk a few steps without the walker but still had vertigo and the general feeling of being off balance. A corpsman removed the braces from his teeth. They had served their purpose and were bothering Gunnar.

CHAPTER

22

Gunnar woke up first on the morning of July 24, the fourteenth day of his trip. He was cooking breakfast when Abigail scooted out of her tent. It looked like it would be a beautiful day for their layover in Joyce Lake.

"Good morning, Abigail," he greeted. "Have a seat. Breakfast is just about ready and I have a cup of coffee for you."

They were both hungry, so the meal of scrambled — from dehydrated — eggs, bacon and stewed fruit were quickly consumed. There were white, puffy clouds in the sky and a gentle breeze was blowing them in a westerly direction. Gunnar spotted two canoes coming from the north end of Joyce heading for the portage into Marj Lake, where they would be going tomorrow.

"Are you interested in going fishing later today?" he asked Abigail. "It would be nice to pick up some walleyes for supper. When my wife and I camped here years ago, we had great walleye fishing."

"I'm not much of a fisherman, Gunnar," Abigail demurred. "Why don't you go? I need to work on my journal and do some laundry. You mentioned yesterday you served in the Marine Corps. What was it like? Were you in Vietnam?"

"I don't really like to talk about it, Abigail," he said. "Talking about it brings back a lot of bad memories. But, yes, I did two tours in Vietnam and I can say that, for most of the men and women who served over there, it was a bad experience."

"I understand your reluctance, Gunnar," Abigail empathized. "I remember when I was growing up in Toronto hearing a lot about American deserters and draft resisters who moved to Canada to avoid having to go to Vietnam. I'm proud of you for your service."

"Thank you," Gunnar replied, touched by her seemingly genuine sincerity.

"Okay," Abigail said after a moment during which neither of them seemed to know what to say next. "I, um, brought along a deck of cards. Would you be interested in playing rummy or maybe cribbage?"

Gunnar thought that was a great idea, so they used Abigail's upturned canoe for a table and played three games of rummy. He was impressed by her card playing. After she beat him easily over three games, his sense of self-preservation kicked in and he suggested they switch to cribbage. They didn't have a cribbage board so they improvised and kept score on a page from Abigail's journal. Gunnar shuffled the cards and they drew to see who would deal first, low card winning the deal. Abigail won but before shuffling the cards again she asked him to cut the deck.

"I'm not falling for that old trick, Abigail," he said with a grin. "If I cut the cards, you get two points."

Abigail laughed but didn't try to argue before proceeding to deal six cards to each of them. Since she was the dealer, it was her crib and they each put two cards in the crib, giving her an extra hand. He led first, with an eight card. She countered with a seven and said, "fifteen two," and scored 2 points. The first to score 121 points wins. As with Rummy, they played three games, except this time he won each time. They were so involved with the game they lost track of time and realized they hadn't had lunch.

After lunch, Gunnar got his fishing gear ready. He waited until the sun was low in the sky and then loaded Emma in the stern before paddling a half-mile north of their campsite to a string of small islands. The wind had subsided and the lake was calm. He found a promising spot about 20 meters off the shore and quickly hooked two 18-inch walleyes using a yellow ball jig with an attached Gulp minnow. He put them on his stringer and continued to fish for another hour, landing and releasing six more fish. After filleting the two walleyes on the shore of the island, he put the fresh fillets in a plastic bag and headed back to camp. It was still early; even though the sun had disappeared, the western sky was glowing, a beautiful orange hue. Abigail fixed a side dish of rice and some of the lemonade vodka mix to go along with the fried walleye.

"It's been a good day, Abigail," Gunnar said. His stomach was full and he was feeling truly sated. "I enjoy being with you."

"It has been a good day," Abigail agreed. "One thing that bothers me about a canoe trip, though, is not being able to take a hot shower."

Gunnar shared his technique of using a bucket of hot water and she decided to try it out. He walked down to the lakeshore to give her some privacy while she bathed. After drying off and putting on clean clothes, she walked down to meet him, saying she felt much better.

"Tomorrow, we'll move on to Conmee Lake," he said. "It's a great fishing lake. Plus, it's also one of my favorite lakes. That's where I caught my first big northern pike in the Quetico, way back in 1964."

They were up early on July 25, Day 15 of Gunnar's trip. The sky was overcast and it was warm and humid, suggesting it might start raining soon. They heard thunder off to the west so, after a quick breakfast, they packed up their gear and headed for the portage into Marj Lake. The first portage was a short lift over to a small pond, followed by a 300-meter portage into Marj. It started to mist as they paddled across Marj to the two short portages into Suzanette Lake. They stopped for a lunch break on the first Darkwater River portage. After resting for a while, they paddled into the main body of Suzanette and took the portage on the west bay of Suzanette to Conmee.

It was midafternoon by the time they set up their tents on a beautiful campsite on a west-facing rocky point near the south end of Conmee. Someone had left a metal grate leaning against the fireplace, plus a small stack of beaver wood. There also was a nice sitting log in front of the fireplace. Abigail hung up a line to dry her wet clothes and Gunnar got a fire started for a pot of coffee.

After they got their tents set up and placed the canoes up by the fireplace, they talked about their trip so far. Gunnar said he was feeling much better, and he realized it was true.

"The medication I'm taking, the one that has affected my strength," he began. "It's for prostate cancer."

"Oh," Abigail said, her expression softening. "I'm sorry to hear that. I will pray for the best possible outcome."

"Thank you," Gunnar replied. "Except for this damn cancer, I've been in good health since my last colon surgery."

"That's frustrating," Abigail said. "But don't lose faith or get depressed. Having a positive attitude toward any illness is very important. And it seems to me that you're getting stronger with each passing day."

They sat by the fire, neither saying anything for a while. Finally, Abigail said she was getting hungry and suggested they fix supper. Later, they watched the sun disappear below the horizon as dusk settled in and they could see the stars appearing in the clear sky.

"There is one thing about Vietnam that I am willing to discuss — one positive, as strange as that sounds," Gunnar said as he watched the night sky light up with stars.

"What's that?" Abigail asked, her tone curious but not pushy.

"The devastating effects of exposure to Agent Orange," Gunnar replied. "That's the herbicide used in Vietnam to defoliate the landscape. It contains dioxin, which is toxic to humans. I was in law school when I got interested in the problem. My interest continued when I moved to Duluth and started my law practice in 1978.

"Dioxin is ubiquitous in the environment," he continued. "Most people are exposed by eating foods that are contaminated. The dioxin in the food is absorbed and stored in fat tissue. Fortunately, the amount of exposure, for most people, is not enough to cause a problem. But dioxin also is a by-product of chlorine bleaching wood pulp, and my firm has represented a lot of clients who were exposed through their work in paper mills.

"I always worried that I might have some repercussions from my exposure in Vietnam, but I never had a problem until now. Fortunately, the VA has recognized the problem and provides medical care for veterans like myself who have been affected."

CHAPTER

2 3

Gunnar dreamed that night about Kathleen. She and her folks had flown to San Diego to visit him in the hospital at the end of October. She and Gunnar talked about where his next duty assignment would be after he was discharged from the hospital. Going back to Vietnam was not an option because of his injuries. The doctors told him he also would not be discharged to full duty until his dizziness was under control and he was able to walk unassisted. He still was using a cane for extra support. They wanted him to continue physical therapy at the Camp Pendleton base hospital after he was released. He was assigned to the Headquarters Company at Main Side to be close to the hospital. Colonel John Roberts was the CO of Headquarters Company.

Gunnar's doctors talked to Gunnar about reconstructing his colon to do away with the need for the colostomy. That would be in February 1971. He would probably be in the hospital for a month after surgery. Gunnar told Kathleen he would like to stay in the Marine Corps and was looking at the possibility of going to law school. It would mean extending his enlistment as a member of the Judge Advocate General Corps.

He finally was released from the hospital just before Thanksgiving in November 1970 and given an extended leave until December 28, when he was due to report back to Balboa for a checkup. Before being discharged, he received the Purple Heart Award.

Kathleen and his folks met him at Minneapolis International on November 24. It was unseasonably warm for November. They picked up Antonio at his apartment and headed for Austin. Gunnar was happy to be home again and was feeling pretty good. He still had pain in his pelvis from the fracture, along with persistent dizziness and the hearing loss in his left ear. Kathleen's family drove down from Ely and they all enjoyed the Thanksgiving holiday together. Most of the conversation centered on Gunnar and how happy they were that he was home.

The time passed too quickly for everyone. Kathleen's family returned to Ely on December 1. They dropped Kathleen and Antonio off at the university to finish the semester. Three weeks later, on December 20, Gunnar and his dad drove up to the Twin Cities to pick up Kathleen and Antonio, both of whom had a weeklong Christmas break. It turned out to be a special Christmas for the Hansen family. Gunnar's sisters, Anna and Sara, were home from college. They all helped decorate a 10-foot-tall balsam fir tree that was placed by the front window in the living room. They had an early supper on Christmas Eve: Marie's traditional clam chowder and homemade walnut, apple and cinnamon potica bread. The snow was falling gently as they drove to midnight Mass at St. Augustine's. Instead of going right home after Mass, they drove around town looking at all the Christmas decorations and Nativity scenes that people had set up in their yards. Fatigue had set in by the time they got home. Everyone went to bed except Gunnar and Kathleen, who stayed up and played Christmas music. It was a magical night.

After opening their presents on Christmas morning, Kathleen, Anna and Sara prepared a special breakfast of frittatas, cinnamon rolls, bacon and hot chocolate. While the girls cleaned the dishes, Marie prepared a special Christmas ham that Charlie had received from Hormel. They planned Christmas dinner later in the afternoon. Marie had invited her two brothers, who were still alive and living in Cloquet, to join them for Christmas, but they were unable to make it. A severe snowstorm hit northeastern Minnesota on December 23, which also prevented Kathleen's family from joining them.

After 10:30 a.m. Mass on Sunday, December 27, the Hansens and Kathleen all went to the annual Christmas brunch sponsored by Hormel in the company's executive dining room. Gunnar wore his Service A uniform and received thanks from many of those in attendance.

"Dad," he said quietly. "I'm embarrassed getting all this attention."

"You don't need to be embarrassed," Charlie said. "My friends are aware of what you have been through and are happy to see you survived and are home. We're all really proud of you, son."

"I wish I could stay longer," he said. "I'm going to miss all of you, especially Kathleen. I think this has been the best Christmas I can remember, for many reasons. I can't thank you and Mom enough. I know I survived my injuries through God's good grace and all your prayers. A Navy corpsman on the USS Sanctuary said I must have a powerful guardian angel."

Charlie and Marie drove Kathleen, Gunnar and Antonio back to the cities on Monday morning, December 28. Gunnar had a 10 a.m. flight to San Diego and Kathleen and Antonio had to go back to school. The hardest part of leaving was saying goodbye to Kathleen again. It was like leaving a part of himself behind, they had become so spiritually intertwined.

CHAPTER

24

The sky was overcast on the morning of July 26, the sixteenth day of Gunnar's trip. The dark water of Conmee was quite a contrast from Sark and Joyce.

"Are you interested in doing some fishing today, Abigail?" Gunnar asked. "I'd like to do some casting for northerns along the shore this morning and then see if we can pick up some walleyes later this afternoon."

"I'll go with you if you would like some company but I don't want to fish," Abigail said.

"That's fine," Gunnar replied. "We can leave the dogs in camp. I want to explore the southern part of the lake. If the weather holds, I'd at least like you to try fishing for walleyes later. Once you get one of those fish on your line, you may change your mind about fishing. Even if not, it's a good skill to have."

When they finished their breakfast, Gunnar got the tarp out and set it up over the fireplace like an awning to protect it from any potential rain while Abigail cleaned the dishes. He got the fishing gear ready and attached a Vibrax Blue Fox # 5 lure to his 12-pound test line. Abigail sat on the bow seat and Gunnar paddled west toward Flat Rock Island, where he had first camped more than fifty years ago. He started casting toward the shoreline on the north side of the island, where the portage to Poohbah Lake starts. Abigail scanned the shore with her binoculars while he fished. There was a slight breeze but, otherwise, the water was calm. He got a snag on his first cast, which stirred things up when he retrieved the lure. They drifted slowly in a southerly direction and he started casting again. He got a solid strike after a few minutes and finally reeled in a small northern, which he released. They rounded a point and moved into a small bay, where the portage to William Lake was located. Abigail spotted an eagle's nest and pointed it out to him as he was casting toward a large beaver lodge. The # 5 Vibrax spinner hit the water with a splash. He waited for five seconds and then started to retrieve it when something big grabbed the bait and started pulling the line off the reel. Gunnar adjusted the drag but the line suddenly went slack. He reeled in the line in, just no fish. The lure was okay, though. Then he noticed movement in the water near where he had lost the fish, and he could make out what looked like a large fish swimming near the surface. He tossed the lure almost on top of the fish and had an immediate strike. This time he set the hook more forcefully and spent the next hour battling the monster pike. When the fish finally surfaced next to the canoe, Abigail was just as excited as he was. The canoe had drifted close to the shoreline during the battle. He was able to get the fish partially into his net before having Abigail hold the net while he lifted the fish into the canoe. Then he stood in the shallow water next to the canoe, holding the fish behind the gills while he measured its length and girth. After removing the landing net and the lure, he carefully lifted the fish, put it back in the water and massaged it until it swam away. It was 40 inches long and had a girth of 24 inches.

Gunnar was willing to acknowledge that he was a bit worn out after his battle with the fish, and Abigail helped him paddle back to their camp. Emma and Lizzie were happy to see them. It started raining while they were eating lunch. Abigail decided to take a nap. Gunnar took his canoe down to the shore and washed it out before he and Emma also retreated to their tent for a siesta. He hoped the rain would stop so they could go walleye fishing later. He thought if he could entice Abigail to at least try jigging for walleyes, she would have the thrill of her life when she caught one.

When Gunnar woke up, the rain had stopped but it was still overcast and felt like more rain was on the way. Abigail was sitting on the log in front of the fireplace, drinking tea and writing in her journal.

"Do you feel rested after your nap?" he asked. "If you still have some hot water left, I think I'll have a cup of tea."

When he had his tea in hand and had settled in on the log by the fire, he brought up fishing again.

"When we go walleye fishing later, we'll use a technique called 'jigging.' It's easy to do and I think you'll like it, especially if you catch a couple of fish. Are you okay with giving it a try?"

Abigail closed her journal and set it aside.

"Sure," she finally conceded. "I am willing to try just about anything once, as long as it's not too dangerous."

Gunnar got both of his fishing rods rigged with yellow ball jigs and Grub minnows.

They left Emma and Lizzie again to mind the camp and paddled toward two small islands at the south end of the lake that Gunnar considered his walleye hole. He showed Abigail how to let the jig drop down about 15 feet and then start raising and lowering her rod to create movement of the jig. She startled in surprise when the tip of the rod bent down toward the water and the line started going out.

"Hold the rod securely and adjust the drag like I showed you," Gunnar advised. "Set the hook and start reeling in some line. Whatever you do, don't let go of the rod."

Abigail lost the first couple of fish that took her bait but she was able to bring the next four to Gunnar's net. They were beautiful 18- to 20-inch walleyes. Gunnar kept an 18-inch and a 20-inch fish for their supper and released the other twelve they caught over the next hour.

It was exciting for both of them. It started to drizzle as they paddled back to their camp. Abigail got a fire going while Gunnar cleaned the fish. They sat on the log under the tarp as they ate the fried walleye and watched the last rays of the sunset through the misty air.

Abigail said she was chilly, even though they were sitting in front of the fire, so Gunnar fixed her a cup of hot chocolate to help warm her. They didn't say much, just listened to the raindrops falling on the tarp. Emma and Lizzie were sitting on the ground next to them. Abigail kept nodding off, so Gunnar walked her to her tent. He stayed up for a while, watching the dying fire before Emma followed him to bed. He said his nightly prayers and fell asleep, dreaming about heading to McIntyre Lake in the morning.

The rain stopped during the night. Their tents and tarp were dry by mid-morning on July 27, the seventeenth day of Gunnar's trip. The route to McIntyre was relatively easy, with just three short portages from Conmee to Brent to McIntyre. It was very warm and humid as they crossed the main body of McIntyre to a small bay on the southwest corner of the lake. Gunnar was relieved when they passed through the narrows and paddled to the southern end of the bay to find the campsite empty. This is where he and Kathleen had stayed for five days on their honeymoon.

It was a large campsite with a 25-meter-long smooth granite landing area and a stand of tall pines that carpeted the smooth ground with their fallen needles. About 30 meters north of the landing area was a small gurgling waterfall where water from the bay formed McIntyre Creek, which flowed south about three-fourths of a mile into Robinson Lake. It was 4- or 5-feet wide in places and populated by frogs and minnows. It also formed the back side of the campsite.

They were both hungry, since they had not had lunch. Gunnar

heated some water for tea while Abigail sliced some Swiss cheese and opened their last box of crackers. She noticed how clear the water was compared to the dark water of Conmee and decided to go swimming after lunch to cool off. Gunnar set up both tents and then paddled across the bay to pick up some beaver wood from an old beaver lodge. Abigail brought her Thermarest mat and towel down to the landing area and, while she dried off in the fading sunlight, they talked about the rest of their trip.

"I would like to stay here in this campsite for three nights," Gunnar said. "This spot is the goal of my trip; it has special meaning to me. Kathleen and I spent our honeymoon here in July 1972, forty-six years ago. I don't think I'll ever make it back here again."

"I'm fine with that, Gunnar," Abigail agreed. "What's the plan after that?"

"From here, we'll take one portage to Sarah Lake and stay there one night. The next day we'll camp in North Bay on Basswood Lake for one night and then head home to Moose Lake."

"I like this place, Gunnar," Abigail said, looking around the campsite. "I think spending a few days here will give us a chance to get rested for the final push to Moose Lake."

They decided to fix supper — beef stroganoff and chocolate pudding — before it got dark. By the time they finished eating and washed the dishes, they noticed a yellow glow of light in the eastern sky. It wasn't long before the full buck moon appeared above the tree tops and slowly ascended, illuminating their camp almost as bright as daylight. It was breathtaking to watch as they sat there entranced by the moon and billions of stars that completely filled the heavens. After a while they got a small fire going and heated some water for tea. Abigail had some cookies she had been saving and they ate those with their tea.

Gunnar said he felt the canoe country held a deeper meaning than just the lakes and trees.

"When I'm on a canoe trip, I feel like I'm in a different world," he said. "This is a place of solitude, devoid of the noise of the modern world, where I can observe the hand of God up close. There are times when I can see and feel the presence of those who have been here before. This happened to me earlier in my trip, when I was camped on Keats Lake. I saw Kathleen seated in front of the campfire laughing. When I approached her to kiss her, the vision was gone. A day never passes when I don't stop what I'm doing and think about this beautiful place and how much I miss it. It's always difficult to make the transition back to civilization when the canoe trip ends."

CHAPTER

2 5

Gunnar lay awake in his tent for a long time after going to bed. He could hear Abigail in her tent, occasionally snoring or making some indistinct sound. For whatever reason, his thoughts drifted to his trip back to the naval hospital in San Diego after spending Christmas at home in 1970. It had been difficult to leave Kathleen. When he returned to Camp Pendleton in January, he made an appointment with the CO of Headquarters Company, Colonel John Roberts.

"Please sit down, Lieutenant Hansen," Colonel Roberts said. "I reviewed your service records ahead of our meeting and want to commend you for your outstanding actions in Vietnam."

"Thank you, sir," Gunnar replied "I wanted to meet with you in person to discuss my future as a Marine. I am scheduled to have another surgery at Balboa in February. When I was wounded in September, part of my colon had to be removed and a colostomy was created. The doctors at Balboa are planning to remove the colostomy and reconnect my bowel. They said I will need to remain in the hospital for a month to make sure everything heals properly. They also expect my balance problem to resolve. If so, they have assured me that I will eventually be able to return to active duty, though I would not be qualified for combat. I have decided I would like to stay in the Marine Corps, though, and attend law school and join the Marine Corps Judge Advocate General Division."

"I would be happy to recommend you for law school, Lieutenant Hansen," Colonel Roberts assured. "Provided you get full medical clearance."

"Yes, sir," Gunnar said. "Thank you, sir."

Gunnar's surgery was on February 10 and he was discharged from the hospital in mid-March to return to limited duty. It took two more months of physical therapy at the base hospital to completely regain his balance before he was cleared in May 1971 for active duty. He passed the Law School Admission Test in April and was accepted to the University of Minnesota Law School for the August 1971 semester. On July 29, he received orders to proceed to Minneapolis for law school, which started on August 8.

Kathleen met him at the airport on July 31. She was anxious to tell him that she would be starting her residency in otolaryngology at U of M in August. It was an exciting time for them. For the first time in four years, they would be together for an extended period. Gunnar rented an apartment in Prospect Park and bought a used Ford F-150 with four-wheel drive.

"Kathleen, now that we are going to be together here in Minneapolis for at least the next three years, why don't we plan to get married next year, when we're on summer break?"

"I think that's a great idea, my dear," Kathleen agreed excitedly. "I'll call my mom and she can start making arrangements. I want to get married at St. Anthony's Catholic Church in July and go on a canoe trip for our honeymoon."

Gunnar would never forget that special time. They were married on a beautiful, sunny day, July 8, 1972. His brother, Antonio, was his best man and Kathleen's sister, Elsa, was her maid of honor. The wedding reception was held at Ely Community Center. Kathleen's mom was able to hire a popular polka band, Bennie Kowalska and the Jumping Polka Bears. Her mom's friends prepared all the food and her dad supplied the beer and wine, along with a bartender from the Yugoslav Home bar. They left the reception after dinner and her dad drove them out to Burntside Lodge, about 8 miles south west of Ely on Burntside Lake. Kathleen wanted to spend their first night as a married couple in cabin No. 26, a beautiful and historic one-room cabin situated away from the main lodge on a rocky point. It's a rustic cabin, popular enough that it usually was reserved for months in advance. Because the Anderssons were good friends of the folks who owned Burntside Lodge, they were able to book the cabin for one night. Gunnar and Kathleen made it a special one.

They went back to Kathleen's home the next day to get their gear ready for their honeymoon canoe trip. A motorboat tow from Moose Lake took them all the way to Washington Island in Basswood Lake. They camped in North Bay and made it to McIntyre the next day.

Gunnar's three years of law school passed by quickly and they found themselves separated again. Gunnar had to attend Navy Justice School in Rhode Island for ten weeks after he finished law school in May 1974. His next duty station was the Judge Advocate General office at Camp Pendleton until June 1978. He was able to take extra leave time to come back to Minneapolis to be with Kathleen and was there when their first child, Lucas, was born in October 1974.

Just before they moved to Duluth in 1978, their second child, Agnes, was born in April. Fortunately, their folks really helped a lot with taking care of Lucas while Kathleen was in her residency and Gunnar was at Camp Pendleton.

26

Emma's barking roused Gunnar from sleep on the morning of July 28. Then he heard Lizzie barking. He called out to Abigail to see if she was awake and if she knew what was going on. He unzipped the tent flap and Emma jumped out of the tent about the same time Abigail let Lizzie out. They heard a ruckus in the woods behind their tents by the stream, and what sounded like branches breaking. The dogs were back there, barking at something moving around in the woods. In a few minutes, Gunnar saw a large bull moose emerge and cross the creek about 30 meters south of their camp. It continued to walk toward the lake, stumbling as it moved, like it was off balance or disoriented. It stopped briefly and looked their way before continuing on.

"Abigail, we need to get the dogs away from the moose as fast as we can," he instructed. "The moose views the dogs as predators, like wolves, and may attack the dogs by kicking them or stomping on them, and may attack us if he is harassed. Emma! Emma! Come here . . . Emma!"

Abigail began calling Lizzie and, after a moment, both dogs came running back to camp.

"Good girls," Abigail praised them. "Let's get you a treat for being so protective. And for coming when we called." She walked over to a pack and began rummaging for the dog treats. "Are we going to be okay, Gunnar?"

"Yes, I think we'll be fine," he said. "The moose seems to have moved on. I'm glad the dogs are trained so well and came when we called them. Moose are different from deer. They typically aren't afraid of humans, so they won't run away from you."

When all the excitement had died down and the dogs were happily munching on their treats, Abigail went back to her tent to get dressed while Gunnar got a fire going. Other than the humidity, it looked like it was going to be a beautiful day, the eighteenth day of Gunnar's trip. After coffee, oatmeal and hard tack biscuits, Abigail said she felt calmer and her pulse had returned to normal. She wondered if there was anything wrong with the moose, since it seemed to be off balance.

"It's hard to say," Gunnar replied. "He was moving pretty fast and the ground may have been uneven. There have been some reports of a brain worm parasite that moose get from eating infected snails and slugs. The snails and slugs get it from infected deer feces. Deer are resistant to the parasite but act as the host in the brain worm life cycle. Moose aren't resistant. The brain worm travels to their spinal cord and brain, which causes imbalance and ultimately death. Some of the ongoing research has suggested that as much as 25% of the decrease in the moose population in northern Minnesota in the past few years may be due to the brain worm parasite."

"That's horrible." Abigail shuddered.

"It is," Gunnar agreed before changing the topic. "Why don't you pack something we can take for lunch and I'll get the fishing gear ready. There is a lake just to the west of this bay that I would like to explore, see if we can catch some bass. Or, rather, see if you can catch some bass. I'm going to paddle and you're going to fish. We'll leave Emma and Lizzie here to guard the camp."

"I'm not sure about that, Gunnar," Abigail said. "Is it like walleye fishing?"

"There is a difference, but I'm going to teach you how right now," Gunnar responded. "The spinning rod and reel is really quite easy to use. I taught all of my kids when they were very young. And you've already had some experience in Conmee fishing for walleyes."

Abigail caught on to the spinning reel technique quickly, though she had trouble remembering to always pull down the bail before casting out the line. Not a major problem but frustrating. They paddled about a mile to the north, to the end of their bay, where there was a small waterfall on the west shore. From there, they had to carry the canoe about 10 meters uphill to the lake where they planned to fish.

"I'll keep the canoe parallel to the shoreline, Abigail," Gunnar said once they were back in the water. "You just cast toward the shore. When your lure hits the water, let it sit there for about three seconds, then start to retrieve it at a moderate pace."

Gunnar put a black Jitterbug on Abigail's line and she started casting. They both wore their sunglasses and hats as some protection against the sunlight glaring off the water. There wasn't much wind, so they moved along slowly. Abigail got a strike on her fifth cast but lost the fish. After a few more casts but no hits, Gunnar changed the lure to a yellow River2Sea Whopper Plopper, after which Abigail caught and released sixteen nice-sized greenback largemouth bass over the next three hours. It started to cloud over, which was a relief from the hot sun, though it remained hot and humid.

"I'm getting tired, Gunnar, and my arm is starting to get sore," Abigail finally said. "I'm not used to casting. I'm also getting hungry."

"Let's stop and have lunch, then," Gunnar agreed. "There's a nice campsite directly across from the waterfall on the east shore of our bay. There used to be a log table there that someone had built."

The log table was still there as Gunnar remembered it, though it was starting to decay. They drank a whole quart of lemonade between them and mixed another one to go with their lunch of soup and crackers.

"I first stayed in this campsite when I was a Boy Scout on a Sommers Canoe Base trip. Mark Spencer was our guide. He was a great guy; he told us a lot of neat stories and had a strong commitment to preserving the wilderness. We'll be fishing for walleyes later today in the place he shared with us on that trip."

The dogs were napping under the shade of some white pines but jumped up to meet them when they landed the canoe back at their campsite.

"It's too early to fish for walleyes," Gunnar told Abigail. "I'm going to take a nap and wait until later to go fishing."

"I think I'll nap, too, Gunnar, but I've had enough fishing," Abigail said. "Besides, I need to catch up on my journal. If you go out later for the walleyes, I can get everything else ready for dinner. The way the sky looks, and with the heat and humidity, we may be in for some rain later today."

Both Gunnar and Abigail slept for a couple of hours before waking to the sound of the wind blowing through the trees.

"It's too windy to go fishing," Gunnar noted when they stepped out of their respective tents, "and it looks like a storm is on the way. If you could help me get the tarp positioned over the fireplace, then we can make sure our tents are tied down."

Once their tents were secure, Gunnar brought both canoes up by their tents and stowed all their loose gear so it was protected from the wind. As they ate dinner, it started to rain, not hard, but steady. They cleaned their dishes and put them back in the proper pack and put the packs under the two canoes, each of which was tied to a tree.

"I still have a few cookies left in my personal pack, Gunnar," Abigail said when they had finished the various tasks involved in securing the camp from the potential storm. "Why don't you heat some water and let's have tea and cookies before we turn in. It looks like the rain could last all night. I think I just heard thunder off to the west."

Before Gunnar could respond, a bolt of lightning shot across the western sky, followed by a loud crash of thunder and then a recurring combination of the two over the next twenty minutes. The rain started and continued in an onslaught with no sign of slowing down. Gunnar's CO in Vietnam had called this kind of rain, "a gully washer," and he wasn't wrong. Gunnar and Abigail said a hasty "good night" and darted to their respective tents with their furry companions.

The sound of the wind and the rain was loud but Gunnar yelled over it to ask Abigail if her tent was dry. He could barely hear her response but he thought she said she was okay. Even with his own dry tent, it was a restless night for Gunnar. He would fall asleep only to have a clap of thunder wake him. He also could hear trees in the distance, falling from the wind.

The storm didn't seem to bother Emma, who was curled up and sleeping soundly at the foot of his sleeping bag.

When Gunnar woke up, the sun was shining; it was cooler and the humid air was gone. It was July 29, the nineteenth day of his trip. He noticed one end of the tarp over the fireplace had come loose but their tents had both weathered the storm. A tree that had blown over had landed on the bow of Abigail's canoe, causing a crack in the hull. Together they moved the tree off the canoe and carried it to the fireplace, where they could better inspect it. Abigail was upset but Gunnar reassured her. He had a special waterproof tape that he could use to patch it. The crack was about 10-inches long on the port side of the canoe at the level of the bow thwart. He suggested they let the canoe dry in the sunlight before he patched it. Abigail could take it to the Souris River factory in Atikokan when she got home from her trip and they could repair it properly.

The cool air was a nice change from the heat and humidity of the past few days. They spent the rest of the day talking and napping and just taking it easy. Gunnar shared a poem with Abigail that he had written some years before,

"Wilderness Day"

"I heard the water softly lapping
Up against the rocky shore and sensed
The gentle breeze upon my face as I lay napping
'Neath the fading sunlight, and all was quiet.

The sky above so pure and blue,
With scattered cotton puff-like clouds.
The only sound, the wind blowing thru
The branches of the white pines 'round my tent.

How can I describe the feeling of that day?
The sense of serenity that all is well.
And if it were possible, I would rather stay
Here in the wilderness forever."

"That poem captures how I feel about this place, Gunnar," Abigail said when he was done reciting it. "Thanks for sharing it with me."

"You're welcome," he said. "So, how would you like to have some fresh walleye for supper? I'm going to head over the narrows — where the walleye cache is — about 4:30 and see if I can catch a few."

He loaded Emma in the stern of his canoe and paddled the half-mile to the narrows. Using a Rapala Shad Rap # 7 lure, he caught fifteen 18- to 20-inch walleyes and kept three of them, enough for two meals. He cleaned them across the bay from their camp and picked up more firewood from the beaver lodge. The fresh fried walleye with rehydrated corn and peas was just the thing with hot tea. They salted the extra fillets, wrapped them in foil and put them in a plastic bag to take to Sarah for dinner the next night.

27

They were up early on July 30th, the twentieth day of Gunnar's trip. They had their gear packed and ready to go by 10 o'clock. The portage from McIntyre to Sarah was about 150 meters long. As they unloaded, Gunnar told her about the portage.

"The first two-thirds is flat and easy," he said. "The last third is a 50-degree slope down to the lake. It seems intimidating when you first see it, but the trick is to go sideways when descending or ascending, using the protruding rocks for footholds."

After he reminded her it may be slippery because of the recent rain, it took them about forty-five minutes to navigate the trail.

Sarah was a beautiful lake. The water was clear and there were a lot of good campsites. They encountered a mild headwind as they paddled into the main body of the lake. They headed south through a narrow area between the east side of a big island and the main-land and found a nice campsite on the mainland. They pulled their canoes up on a smooth, rocky shelf that was the landing area and set the packs next to a small fireplace that Gunnar remembered from the last time he was there. After setting up their tents, they had lunch.

"This will be our last chance to go fishing, Abigail," he said. "I've heard that Sarah has lake trout. This is not the best time of the year for them, but it might be fun to give it a try. I'll paddle and you can fish, like we did in McIntyre, except you'll be trolling the lure. If we don't latch on to a laker, we could possibly tie into a big northern pike."

"That sounds fine," Abigail said. "What do I have to do?"

"It's easy," Gunnar reassured her. "Number one, keep a good grip on the rod and stay alert. If a fish takes your lure, you don't want it to jerk the rod out of your hands. Second, you want to set the hook by pulling back on the rod. Third, you have to adjust your drag to try to slow the fish down without breaking the line. I think you'll know what to do when the time comes. The lure I'm putting on the line is a Doctor Spoon 285. It weighs about one and a half ounces and will sink down as I paddle. I attached a swivel, too, to help to keep the line from twisting."

They paddled south from their campsite around the point of the big island and headed west toward the opposite shore about 2miles away. Abigail dropped the Spoon into the lake and opened the bail to allow the line to go out.

"I think that's enough," Gunnar said. "Close the bail and set the drag. I'm not sure how deep it is here. If you feel the lure bumping on the bottom, you know you're deep enough."

They wore their sunglasses and hats to thwart the sun's glare and Gunnar paddled slowly into a mild headwind. It was a beautiful day. They were both commenting on the weather when Abigail startled as her rod began bouncing up and down and the tip went into the water. The reel started singing as the line was disappearing into the clear water.

"Increase the drag, Abigail!" Gunnar instructed. "You have a fish. Hold the rod tight and hang on. Don't panic. Try to reel in some line, but don't rush things. You have to play the fish."

"Oh, Gunnar, my heart is racing as fast as the line is going into the water," Abigail said. "Maybe you should take the rod."

"Not a chance, Abigail," Gunnar disagreed. "This is your fish and I know you can handle it. Just keep the line tight and hold on to the rod. The fish will eventually tire; be patient. This is the moment every fisherman lives for: the thrill of the struggle between you and the fish. Win or lose, once you've experienced it, you'll never forget it and you can't wait until you can experience it again. You didn't know what you've been missing until now, did you?"

The fish kept pulling out more line, even as Abigail increased the drag. After a few minutes, she was gradually able to retrieve some line, only to have it go out again. Her rod kept bending and she had trouble keeping the tip out of the water.

"My arms are getting sore, Gunnar," she eventually said, though the excitement in her tone was far from exhausted. "I just hope I can hang on."

Gradually, though, she began to win the battle and it wasn't too long before she started reeling in line. The fish soon surfaced next to the canoe.

"That's a beautiful lake trout you've caught," Gunnar praised. "Keep the line tight and point your rod back toward me so I can get the fish in the landing net. The spoon is hooked in its upper lip. You're lucky it didn't pull out. You did a great job catching this one Abigail."

He measured the length of the fish and then carefully put it back in the water, holding on to it until it was able to swim away. They were both feeling effects of the adrenalin rush they had just experienced and decided to head back to their camp to recover and maybe have an early supper.

"That was a beautiful 32-inch lake trout, Abigail," Gunnar said. "I've never caught one that large."

Gunnar mixed the last of the lemonade and vodka and helped Abigail cook the leftover walleye from McIntyre and the last of the freeze-dried rice. Hot tea and instant butterscotch pudding for dessert topped off the meal.

"I have to say, Abigail, this has been one of the most memorable and enjoyable canoe trips I think I've ever taken," Gunnar said. "You've been a good companion and I probably owe my life to you for saving me back on Sark. And I'm so happy for you for catching the lake trout."

"I'm happy we've had this time together, Gunnar," Abigail replied. "I never understood what a remarkable man you are until now. Looking back on your life, you have accomplished so much that you're not even aware of. I will miss seeing you all the time when our trip ends, but I will see you again. Where I come from, we don't do any fishing or canoeing, so this trip has been a special time for me."

"It's nice of you to say such kind words, Abigail," Gunnar said, feeling just a bit embarrassed. "I think you may be exaggerating things a bit. I know I feel physically and emotionally much better than I did three weeks ago, and I think you've had something to do with that. When I first saw you on Sark Lake, you reminded me of a Navy corpsman I met in Vietnam. He saved my life three times. You kind of look like him. Could he have been related to you, maybe your father or an older brother?"

"I don't think so; I've been told I look like a lot of people," Abigail said.

"I just thought I'd ask," Gunnar replied. "Let me help with the dishes, then I'm going to get all the fishing gear packed so we can get going early in the morning. The first portage out of Sarah will be challenging. It's 630 meters uphill to Side Lake. Then we have two or three mucky but shorter portages to Isabella Lake. From Isabella, we'll travel about a mile in a beaver stream into a small lake that is usually covered with white and yellow lily pads. Then to North Bay of Basswood Lake. From there, we have a 6-mile paddle south through North Bay to the campsite where we'll stay tomorrow night."

Abigail said good night to Gunnar and she and Lizzie retired to their tent. Gunnar made sure the packs were stowed under his canoe. It was still light out when Gunnar and Emma got into their tent. Even so, he was asleep almost as soon as he crawled into his sleeping bag.

Abigail's clock was set to wake them at 7 a.m.

CHAPTER

28

———————

Gunnar was up before Abigail's alarm started ringing. The sky was overcast and it looked like it might rain. Gunnar had coffee and oatmeal ready for Abigail when she got out of her tent, and they were loading their canoes by 8:30. That's when the rain started. It was July 31, the twenty-first day of Gunnar's trip. Gunnar struggled on the portage into Side Lake, which still took three trips, even with Abigail's help. In all, it took them two hours to traverse the three portages from Side to Isabella, the drizzling rain their constant companion. Gunnar slipped on one of the muddy portages into Isabella and dropped his canoe. It was humiliating, but he got up and flipped the canoe back onto his shoulders and finished the portage. Once they got to Isabella, it was much easier going. The rain finally stopped as they were paddling northeast on Isabella.

The 90-meter portage from Isabella to the beaver stream was congested by a group of Scouts from Sommers Canoe Base. These were the first people they had seen since Joyce Lake. They were a noisy but friendly bunch who said they were headed to Sarah Lake. It was a mixed group of six teenage boys and girls with their adult male chaperone and a female guide. Once the group cleared out and was on its way to Isabella, Gunnar and Abigail carried their gear over the portage.

"It sure is different at the canoe base from when I guided there back in the 1960s," Gunnar said. "I can't imagine mixing teenage boys and girls together on a canoe trip with all those hormones struggling to get out of the corral like a herd of wild horses. It reminds me of the Cole Porter song, 'Anything Goes.' Our culture sure has changed."

They paddled with the current through the beautiful, serpentine, mile-long beaver stream and finally made it to what Gunnar called Lily Pad Lake, a shallow 60-acre body of water with white and yellow lily pads covering half of its surface.

"This is beautiful, Gunnar," Abigail gasped. "But . . . I don't want to damage the flowers with my paddle."

"Don't worry, Abigail," Gunnar reassured her. "These lily pads are tough. They keep coming back every year, in spite of all the canoe traffic. When I'm here, I feel like I'm in one of Monet's famous lily pad paintings. I don't know any place like it anywhere else in the park."

They had two or three beaver dams to pull over and a short portage to take before they were finally in North Bay. It was midafternoon and they stopped to have lunch before the final 6-mile paddle to the cedar grove campsite where Gunnar planned to camp.

The first thing Abigail noticed when they finally got to their campsite in the late afternoon was the pleasant odor of the cedar trees.

"I love the cedar fragrance," she said. "It feels so cozy here, being inside a protective wall of cedar trees. This is definitely a special place."

"I'm glad you like it," Gunnar replied. "It is a special place, for a number of reasons. Kathleen and I camped here on the first night of our honeymoon. And the cedar trees enhance its uniqueness and beauty."

"It doesn't look like anyone has been here for a long time, though," Abigail said, looking around. "The fireplace is starting to fall apart. How about I rearrange the rocks to get them back in place while you gather some firewood?"

They set up their tents and got a fire going using cedar branches that had fallen to the ground. Gunnar brewed a pot of coffee and they each had a cup before fixing the last of their freeze-dried mac and cheese and chocolate pudding. They sat on a log in front of the fire and talked about their plans for tomorrow.

"If the weather is halfway decent, we should be able to make it to Moose Lake by midafternoon," Gunnar said. "Why don't we stop at the canoe base first. You can call LaTourell's Resort from there."

"I wonder if they still have my reservation on file," Abigail mused. "My daughter was supposed to make the reservation. I hope she didn't forget to do it."

"If you don't have a reservation we can probably stay at the base. I'll call my son, Lucas, and he can drive up from Duluth to pick us up. He has a double canoe rack for his car so he can handle both canoes."

"That sounds fine, Gunnar," Abigail agreed. "I'll call my daughter and let her know I'm back and she won't have to pick me up."

At that moment the sun disappeared behind the trees lining United States Point, which was a mile directly across from their campsite, and the sky was filled with yellow, gold and orange. Two canoes were passing U.S. Point, heading south, the same direction they'd be heading in the morning. Gunnar carried both of their canoes up by his tent and put their packs under his. Abigail said she was tired and was going to bed.

"It's been fun," she said. "Take care. Good night, Gunnar."

"I will, Abigail. Don't forget to set your alarm. See you in the morning."

Gunnar stayed up and watched the fire burn down before he and Emma went to bed.

CHAPTER

2 9

August 1, the twenty-second day of Gunnar's trip, was a most unusual day. Gunnar and Emma were awakened by the sound of people talking and paddles bumping against aluminum canoes. He initially thought he was dreaming before it registered that the sounds were very real. He unzipped his tent flap and made it outside just in time to see four Alumacraft canoes passing by their campsite, headed into North Bay. He wondered if Abigail had heard the people talking as they passed by and then wondered why he hadn't heard her alarm go off. He called her name and looked over to her tent, but it was gone.

In fact, everything associated with Abigail was gone: her tent, her packs, her canoe, Lizzie. Abigail herself. He was all alone again, except for Emma. The clean dishes and pots from last night were still on top of his canoe where he had placed them. He checked the food pack under his canoe. All of his food supplies, what was left of them, were there but all of her food was gone.

Gunnar didn't know what to think. He couldn't understand how she could have packed up all of her stuff and left without either Emma or him hearing anything. It didn't make any sense. He decided the only thing to do was to pack up and head for Moose Lake. As he paddled away from the campsite, his strokes had a bit more power behind them, fueled by his befuddlement and, yes, anger over Abigail's disappearance.

The wind was blowing gently from the northeast as Gunnar paddled the 6 miles south in Basswood Lake to Wind Bay, which was on the Minnesota side of the international border. It took about three hours of steady paddling to get to the 850-meter portage to Wind Lake. He had to stop at Washington Island and add some rocks to the bow of the canoe to help the balance, since his food pack was nearly empty. A rumble in his stomach reminded Gunnar that he had not eaten breakfast, so he had some rye crisp crackers and honey and the last of the trail mix before he started the portage. He made it in three trips.

He had to deal with a mild head wind as he paddled the 3 miles east across Wind Lake to the 800-meter portage to Moose Lake. He missed having Abigail's help, especially now, as he contemplated whether he could muster the strength to get over this final portage. The sun was making its afternoon descent as he carried the last of his gear to the Moose Lake end of the portage. It had taken three trips — and some pain meds for his aching back and shoulders — but he finished and rested his canoe in Moose Lake.

Moose Lake was calm except for a few motor boats that were coming and going from the resorts and outfitters at the lake's south end. The wake from the outboard motors could be disruptive to canoeists but, by and large, there was a certain mutual respect in most cases. The canoe base was on the east side of Moose, almost directly across from the Wind Lake portage. Gunnar unloaded his gear onto the Sommers dock and placed it next to his canoe, which he put on a nearby canoe rack. No one was around, so he and Emma followed a wide gravel-filled path up the hill to the main lodge, which he remembered from when he guided there.

There were a lot of Scouts — boys and girls — in their uniforms milling around. His plan was to ask if Bridgett Olson was available, or at least see if he could stay at the base for the night, until he could get Lucas or one of his daughters to drive up to Ely and give him a ride back to Duluth. He must have stood out in his grubby canoeing outfit because a neatly dressed young man in a Scout uniform and with a "Staff" badge approached Gunnar.

"Hello, sir," he said. "I'm Dave Hagen, the guide chief. Can I help you?"

"Dave, glad to meet you," Gunnar held out his hand to shake. "I'm Gunnar Hansen. I used to be a guide here many years ago. I just completed a three-week canoe trip this afternoon and wound up here. I'm hoping I can stay here overnight until I can get someone from my family to pick me up tomorrow. Actually, I was hoping Bridgett Olson might be here, too. I met her about two weeks ago on Sturgeon Lake."

"Very happy to meet you, Gunnar. Yes, Bridgett told me about meeting you. She was very impressed by you and told me to be on the lookout for you. She just returned from a trip yesterday and was planning to take a few days off, but she may still be here. Let me see if I can have one of the staff try to find her. Meanwhile, Gunnar, you must be hungry. Where did you leave your canoe and packs?"

"Everything is down at the waterfront."

"Let's bring it up here to the lodge so it doesn't get lost," Dave suggested. "With all these people roaming around, things have a tendency to disappear, especially fishing rods and paddles."

Dave talked to a couple of Scouts who were nearby and we all walked down to the waterfront. Dave and the two Scouts carried my stuff up to the Lodge and put it in his office.

"We'll keep your stuff safe in there until you leave," he said. "I'm going to get you a clean towel and some soap so you can shower. Then we'll head up to the dining hall and you can get something to eat. Bridgett should be here before too long. The word is she's in a meeting with the base director."

Bridgett finally caught up with Gunnar when he and Dave were in the dining hall. She gave him a big hug and said how happy she was to see him. Dave excused himself and left them alone to talk.

"So how was your trip?" she asked. "You look better than when I saw you last, in Sturgeon."

"Well, I survived, as you can see," Gunnar smiled before turning more serious. "At one point, I was quite ill. On Sark Lake. I was more or less rescued by a kind lady who happened to be camping where I was planning to camp. We traveled together for a few days after that but then we split up, and I came on to Moose Lake by myself. Taking those two portages from Wind Bay today just about did me in. Anyway, I'm happy to be back and very happy to see you, Bridgett."

"I called your son Robert to tell him I was with you on Sturgeon," she said. "We had a nice conversation and we're going to get together in Madison later this week. I have to go there tomorrow for a few days to take care of some business at the school where I teach, but I'll be coming back to the base to guide one more trip later this month."

"I need to call my son Lucas and ask him if he can come up here tomorrow to haul me back to Duluth."

"Don't worry about it, Gunnar," Bridgett said. "Use the phone in the office to call Lucas and tell him I will drive you to Duluth on my way to Madison. We have a place for you to sleep tonight in one of the guest cabins. We've kind of been expecting you."

CHAPTER

3 0

The next morning, August 2, they loaded Gunnar's canoe on top of Bridgett's car and put his gear in the trunk. They stopped at LaTourell's Resort on the way to Ely, but they didn't have any record of a reservation for Abigail Fraser. He had to stop at U.S. Customs in Ely to check in and show his passport. The Customs agent wasn't too friendly and Gunnar was happy when they were finally on their way. From there they stopped by Britton's Cafe on Chapman Street for breakfast. The two-hour drive to Duluth was uneventful and Gunnar gave a silent sigh of relief when they pulled into his driveway. Lucas was waiting for them and gave his dad a hug before thanking Bridgett for bringing him safely home.

Between the three of them, it took almost no time to get Gunnar's stuff unloaded.

Lucas again thanked Bridgett for her help.

"I'm glad to," she replied, "and I'm happy to meet you, Lucas. I should probably get on my way. It's a six-hour drive to Madison and I'm supposed to meet your brother, Robert, for dinner tonight at Lombardino's. It's my favorite Italian restaurant."

"We wouldn't want you to miss that, then," Lucas said with a smile.

"I'll be coming back this way on Sunday." Bridgett met his smile with one of her own. "Robert said he may follow me back, because he wants to visit with you, Gunnar."

"I look forward to seeing you again in a few days, then," Gunnar replied, shaking Bridgett's hand.

"I think the canoe trip must have been therapeutic, Dad," Lucas said as they were turning to go inside after Bridgett's departure. "You look healthier than when you started out three weeks ago. Why don't we have a beer. I'll order your favorite pepperoni pizza from Sammy's in Lakeside. I told Agnes I would call her when you got home."

"That sounds good," Gunnar agreed. "Bridgett and I had coffee and hot cakes for breakfast at Britton's in Ely, but I'm still hungry. I may look better and I *do* feel better, but I think I may have lost a few pounds. I really struggled on some of the portages. I'm happy to be home. It was probably the most interesting canoe trip I've ever taken. . . . By the way, what's going on between Bridgett and Robert?"

"I'm not sure," Lucas replied. "Robert told me they really hit it off when she called him about the progress of your canoe trip, so they decided to get together when she got back to Madison. It will be interesting to see what develops. Anyway, I'm anxious to hear more about your trip."

"I can't wait to tell you all about it, but I'm going to call Dr. Lister's office while we're waiting for the pizza," Gunnar said. "I still have that damn catheter in my bladder and I need to have him take it out. Plus, I want to confirm the scan I'm supposed to have next week."

Agnes and the pizza delivery guy from Sammy's arrived at Gunnar's home at the same time. While Lucas paid for the pizza, she gave her dad an especially big hug.

"I'm so glad you're home," she said. "We worried about you all the time you were gone and said a lot of prayers for you. How do you feel? You look pretty good. Please, tell us about your trip. Over pizza, though — I haven't had lunch yet."

"That's a lot all at once, Agnes," Gunnar laughed. "As I mentioned to Lucas, I am very happy to be home. I missed you all. I had a very memorable canoe trip, unlike any I've experienced in the past. Besides meeting Bridgett and a group of Scouts from the canoe base and sharing a campsite with them, I also met a very fine gentleman, Jack Riley. He was the father of one of the boys in the Scout crew. It turns out that Jack also is the son of my CO when I was on my second tour in Vietnam. But that's another story, and we can talk about that later."

"Well, that answers one question, Dad," Lucas said after swallowing a bite of pizza. "Someone named Jack Riley has been calling the office asking for you. I didn't talk to him but my secretary took a message from him. He wants you to call him as soon as you get back. I was involved in a deposition both times he called and I forgot all about him until you mentioned him."

"That's okay, Lucas," Gunnar said. "He is a very nice man and I will call him back later today. Besides being the son of my CO, he also is a U.S. congressman from Wichita."

"This is good pizza," Agnes said, swallowing her own bite. "I was even hungrier than I thought. So, tell us more about your trip, Daddy."

"Save some pizza for us, Agnes," Gunnar laughed. "Lucas and I are hungry, too. Would you mind getting me another beer?"

Gunnar took a bite of his own slice of pizza, taking his time. He knew he needed to tell his kids everything about his trip, but he wasn't sure how they'd respond to his story about Abigail. After Agnes returned with his beer and settled in, he finally started.

"I did get sick on the trip," he said after a deep breath. "Actually, at one point I wasn't sure I was going to make it. I got hypothermic, nauseated and delirious on the portage into Sark Lake."

"Daddy," Agnes gasped.

"I'm OK," Gunnar pointed out. "Things turned out fine."

"So what happened?" Lucas asked.

"Well, it was raining like crazy and I basically ran out of energy carrying my stuff," Gunnar started. "I thought I was going to die, I felt so bad. When the rain finally stopped, I was barely able to load up the canoe and head for the campsite where I was planning to stay. I don't remember much after that except, somehow, my canoe ended up at the right campsite, and a lady by the name of Abigail Fraser was already camped there."

"Do you mean she rescued you, Dad?"

"Yes, Lucas," Gunnar agreed. "If it had not been for Abigail, I'm not sure I would be here today."

"That's an unreal story," Agnes said. "What happened to Abigail?"

"Well, I asked her if she would stay with me for the rest of my journey, at least until I got to McIntyre, where mom and I spent our honeymoon."

"And did she?" Agnes asked, all curiosity. "Can we meet her sometime?"

"That's what's so weird," Gunnar said. "We spent eleven days together, including three days at the McIntrye campsite, and the plan was for her to travel with me until we got to Moose Lake. She said she had reservations to stay at LaTourell's Resort. Our last camp was at the North Bay cedar grove. She was supposed to set her alarm clock so we could get an early start yesterday morning. I never heard the alarm go off and, when I woke up, she was gone — her tent, her canoe, her dog, and all of her gear."

Lucas and Agnes both tried to talk at once, Lucas finally prevailing.

"She just disappeared?" he asked. "She was gone and left no trace of herself behind? That's crazy. People don't just disappear into thin air. Did anyone else see her? You said she had her own tent — so you didn't share a tent with her?"

Agnes cut in, raising her voice so she could be heard over Lucas. "Is it possible that you just imagined her, when you were delirious?"

Gunnar looked reproachfully at Agnes and Lucas before addressing them as if they were children. They *were* his children, after all.

"I am offended by your suggestion that Abigail Fraser is a figment of my imagination," he scolded. "You should know I would never lie to you or try to deceive you. Not about something like this. She was as real as you two are sitting here with me." He looked specifically at Lucas. "I'm also offended by your suggestion that I would take advantage of the woman and share a tent with her."

Their father hadn't spoken to them like that in years, and Agnes and Lucas both look suitably chastised.

"We're sorry, Dad," they said, practically in unison before Lucas tacked on a "please accept our apologies."

"We love you very much, Dad," Agnes chimed in. "We're just worried about you."

"Apologies accepted," Gunnar said, his tone losing its sternness. "I love you and your brother and sisters. Never forget that."

"Of course not, Dad," Agnes said.

Gunnar paused for a moment. He wasn't sure how they were going to take what he had to say next.

"If I can be completely honest with you, I'm not sure she was human," he finally admitted.

"What do you mean?" Lucas asked, doing a poor job of concealing his concern.

"Well, it's a long story, one I have never really shared," Gunnar began. "When I was wounded in Vietnam, the same Navy corpsman saved my life three times — once on my first deployment, when I was about to be shot by a VC; and twice when I was wounded in 1970. He was there then to stop me from bleeding from the gunshot wound in my right thigh and from bleeding to death from the more serious wound in my gut.

"For some reason, I remember the face of that corpsman. Abigail Fraser was an attractive woman, but what I noticed most about her was that her face was almost identical to that of the corpsman in Vietnam. I even asked her if she had an older brother or maybe her father who was a corpsman, but she said no. Then she told me people think she looks like a lot of people. She also told me that, where she came from, they didn't do any fishing or canoeing."

"Do you remember anything else about her, Dad?" Agnes asked

"As a matter of fact, there is one other thing that I had forgotten about," Gunnar said, pausing as he recalled the moment. "When I woke up the morning after she rescued me, she was cooking breakfast. When I got out of my tent her first words were, 'Good morning; I've been waiting for you, Gunnar.' I was so confused at the time by what had happened to me the night before that I didn't dwell on her comment — whether she was waiting for me to wake up or waiting for me to show up at her campsite. She said she knew my name from going through my packs and finding my Quetico travel permit. As I think about it now, I can't help but wonder if it was just a coincidence that she was at the campsite where I was planning to stay or if she was really waiting there for me to show up."

Agnes and Lucas looked at each other, clearly baffled and more than a bit concerned by Gunnar's comments.

"I think we should just wait and see if your Abigail shows up," Lucas finally spoke. "If she does, we can ask her about everything. Right now, we don't have any physical proof that she even existed. Robert and Bridgett will be back this weekend and we can get their opinion."

"I agree with Lucas," Agnes said, standing. "For now, I should get going. I have to pick up my kids from school. Thanks for the pizza. I'm happy you're home. We'll figure it out. Maybe she *was* an angel who was there to protect you. Based on your story, she certainly accomplished that task."

"Funny you should mention that, Agnes," Gunnar said, standing to give his daughter a hug goodbye. "I have actually wondered about that possibility myself. I know it sounds far out but, as I look back on my life, there have been many times when I have been rescued, so to speak, by some power or force that kept me safe and alive. You know, the Bible is full of stories of angels sent by God to come to the aid of humans in time of need. I don't think we should dismiss the idea that Abigail may have been an angel."

By the time Agnes and Lucas left, Gunnar was tired. He hadn't slept well the night before at the canoe base. He couldn't relax, wondering what had happened to Abigail. His recent discussion with his two oldest children also had been frustrating. He still wasn't sure if they believed his story. It's too bad he didn't have anything of Abigail's that he could show them or a picture of her. He picked up his bottle of Grain Belt beer and walked into the living room. Once settled into his favorite chair, he promptly fell asleep.

It was dusk out when he was awakened by the phone ringing. It was his daughter Marie. He had just gotten off the phone with her when his daughter Ruth called. Another 10 minutes and the call was from Robert, welcoming him home and letting him know Bridgett had arrived safely in Madison. "You won't believe what a small world this is," Robert said. "Bridgett and I had never met before, but we're almost neighbors here in Madison, and I know her folks. I'll tell you all about it when we see you this weekend. Sorry, I need to go — I'm late picking her up for our dinner date. Love you, Dad!"

Gunnar checked the time. It was 6:30 p.m. He had slept for at least three hours and, despite the earlier pizza, was famished. He took a quick shower, changed clothes and walked across the street to Northland Country Club, where he had a steak dinner as he relaxed into the club's familiarity. He had joined the club when they first moved to Duluth. He wasn't much of a golfer but all the kids learned to swim in the club pool and Kathleen was a low-handicap golfer. The rolling hills of the course also provided for great sledding in the winter.

CHAPTER

3 1

Friday, August 3, dawned bright and sunny. Gunnar had slept well — it was good to be home and in his own bed — and he felt refreshed. He got dressed and he and Emma drove almost to the end of East Superior street, to the New London Cafe, for breakfast. He liked New London because the restaurant had great food and its owners allowed him to bring Emma. He usually tried to make it there two or three times a week for breakfast, a habit he had developed after Kathleen passed away. He was a creature of habit, though not to the point where he got stressed if his routine changed. He wasn't a neat freak, but he *did* like order in his life. He decided the first thing he needed to do when he finished breakfast was to attend to his camping gear, though he didn't have any illusion that he would be going on another canoe trip anytime soon.

His canoe and packs were on the floor of his garage where Lucas and Bridgett had placed them, and Gunnar took a moment to admire his canoe. It had served him very well on his trip. He carefully carried it outside to the backyard and, using a large sponge, scrubbed it clean. He hung his tent, tarp and air mat on a clothesline to air and dry out. The bag of cooking gear was set aside to be rewashed. That took care of one of the Duluth packs.

The stuff in the other Duluth pack — the food pack — was dumped into a large cardboard box. His sleeping bag was set aside to be taken to a dry cleaner's and his clothes were headed for the washing machine, all except for the canvas pants and boots, which were put in a special suitcase along with his belt, suspenders, knife and pliers. His fishing rod case and tackle boxes were stored in a closet in the house, where all the camping equipment would eventually end up.

He was about to go through the stuff in the cardboard box when the garage phone rang. It was an unknown caller and he almost hung up, except he saw the call was coming from Kansas.

"Good morning, Mr. Hansen," a cheery voice on the other end said once pleasantries were out of the way. "I'm calling for Congressman Jack Riley. He's been trying to reach you. Would it be okay if I contact Mr. Riley now and have him call you back at this number in a few minutes?"

"Yes, that would be fine," Gunnar said. "I heard that Jack had called my office and I meant to call him yesterday, but it just didn't happen. I will wait for his call."

"Thank you, sir. Mr. Riley should be calling you in a few minutes. Goodbye."

Gunnar went into the house to wait for the phone to ring again. It did, in just five minutes.

"Hello, Jack," Gunnar said when Jack identified himself. "I'm sorry I didn't call you sooner. I just got home yesterday. I was going to call then, but time got away from me."

"It's fine, Gunnar," Jack replied. "It's good to hear your voice. How was your trip?"

"It was really good," Gunnar said. "I had a great time. How about you?"

"We had a successful trip, too," Jack said. "That Bridgett is really some gal. She was a great guide. She taught us all about wilderness camping. We had some fantastic walleye fishing in Darky Lake. On the way home we picked up a tail wind on Brent and

McIntyre and were able to cross the lakes with wind power using our tarps for sails. The boys are already planning next year's trip."

"It sounds like you had quite a time," Gunnar said. "But I'm guessing you didn't just call to ask about my trip. What can I help you with?"

"I wanted to talk to you about the letter my dad sent to Mom after you were injured in that battle in September 1970. He did recommend you for the Medal of Honor. I'm not sure whether he was overruled by a senior officer or if his recommendation got lost in all the confusion after Dad died. Anyway, I've asked General Higgins, the Marine Corps commandant, to review your service records in conjunction with the Secretary of Defense. If they agree there's good evidence for the Medal of Honor award, I am going to submit a special bill to Congress to approve it. Yours is a special case, Gunnar. Normally, the Medal of Honor must be awarded within three years of the act of valor. It requires Congress to change the rules when we're talking about giving the award forty or fifty years after the fact."

"I appreciate your interest in the matter, Jack," Gunnar said. "I really do. But I'm not sure what I did was extraordinary enough to qualify for the Medal of Honor. Still, I would like to invite you to visit me here sometime and I can show you around Duluth. I am thinking about having a party in a few weeks, to celebrate being home. Maybe you could come for a visit then."

"You let me know when and I will be there," Jack assured. "In the meantime, let's see what happens with the medal. I'll call you as soon as I find out. Take care, Gunnar, and say hi to Bridgett for me."

It wasn't lunchtime yet, but it was hot out and Gunnar got a beer out of the fridge. He made a mental note to get more beer and other groceries tomorrow. He finished the beer and took a few minutes to go through the mail that had accumulated while he was gone. Aside from a few bills, most of it was "junk" mail.

Back in the garage, Gunnar sorted through the stuff in the box. Under the small pile of packages of leftover freeze-dried food, he found his Earl Grey tea and, next to it, a box of Chamomile tea. He blinked at it in confusion before realization dawned. It wasn't his tea. It was Abigail's. It also was evidence that she had been with him, even if there was no way he could prove to his children that he hadn't simply bought a box and put it there himself.

He shook the pack sack, holding it upside down until every bit of debris inside had fallen out. He was just about convinced the bag was truly empty when a leather-bound notebook came tumbling out of the pocket on the front of the pack. He picked it up and recognized it as Abigail's journal. The last entry was dated July 31 and mentioned the cedar grove campsite. He wondered how he had missed seeing the book when he cleaned out the pack initially, but he found a piece of cloth had been wedged in the pocket to keep the book from easily sliding out. He called Lucas, who said he would come by the house as soon as he could get away from his office.

"Whoever did this meant for the book to be found, but not without some effort," Lucas said, looking it over. "The same might be said for the box of Chamomile tea. There's no question in my mind that Abigail exists, but who or what she is and what happened to her is a mystery. I'll let Agnes know. Why don't you talk to Robert and Bridgett when they get here but, otherwise, let's keep it quiet."

Gunnar agreed with that plan.

"I do feel vindicated finding this stuff, though, especially the journal," he said. "What do you think about doing some detective work to see if you can find out anything about her? I'll write down everything I can remember about her and you can use your contacts to ask around."

3 2

Robert and Bridgett arrived from Madison on Sunday afternoon. Gunnar brought them up to date on his canoe trip and his mysterious canoeing partner, Abigail, and then treated them to an early dinner at Northland.

"As I mentioned on the phone, Dad, it was quite a surprise to find that I know Bridgett's folks, though I didn't know Bridgett until she called me to tell me about the progress of your canoe trip," Robert said. "My engineering company has done some design and construction work for her dad's office building. About four years ago, we put an addition on the Edgewood School of the Sacred Heart, where she teaches high school. I remember she was on the planning committee that met with us. And her brother, Bob, is one of my musky fishing buddies."

"Well, I'm happy that you two finally met," Gunnar said. He turned to Bridgett. "Jack Riley called me yesterday — he had nothing but kudos for you and his canoe trip."

"That's very kind of him," Bridgett responded. "They were a great group to be with, highlighted, I might add, by meeting you on Sturgeon. . . . I am going to retire from guiding after this summer, though. I have one more trip later this week. In addition to teaching at Edgewood, they want me to do some administrative work, which will involve working during the summer break."

"It's hard to give up guiding," Gunnar said, "but congratulations on the new responsibilities. I'm sure you'll be great."

"I told her the same," Robert agreed. "So, how are you feeling, Dad? And, the big question, where is Abigail Fraser?"

"I'll answer the easy question first," Gunnar said. "I think I'm better than when you dropped me off at Beaverhouse three weeks ago. My appointment with my urologist is later this week and I'll know more then. As far as Abigail is concerned, I've given Lucas all the information I can remember her telling me about herself and he's going to do some investigating. We'll see where it goes."

When Gunnar woke up on Monday morning, August 6, the fog was so thick he couldn't see his backyard. This happened periodically. It had to do with warm, moist air from the Duluth Heights area on the west side of Duluth coming into contact with the cool ground moisture along the lakefront and raising the dew point. Bingo: fog. The problem resolved itself by mid-morning, helped along by what proved to be bright sun. Gunnar was reading the paper and drinking his second cup of coffee in the kitchen when Robert and Bridgett walked in.

Robert had slept in his old room on the second floor while Bridgett was in Agnes' room on the lower level, which had a private bathroom.

"Good morning," Robert greeted his dad. "We're going over to the park to play tennis. We'll stop someplace for lunch and then we'll be back to pick up our stuff. We're going to drive to Ely and the canoe base this afternoon. She has to leave on a canoe trip on Thursday, so I'm going to hang around until then and then head back to Madison."

Gunnar called Lucas after Robert and Bridgett left for their game.

"Hi, Lucas," he greeted. "I wanted to be sure I mentioned that Abigail said she has a condo here in Duluth and that her daughter also lives in Duluth. We never got around to exchanging phone numbers, and I can't remember her daughter's name. She did say she did volunteer work at St. Benedict's."

"Thanks, Dad," Lucas said. "I think I have all the information I need. I am going to submit the journal to one of my contacts at the police department for a fingerprint check. In the meantime, my secretary is making phone inquiries to the various places where Abigail said she and her late husband worked. I also have a call in to the Souris River canoe factory, to see if they have a sales record for her canoe."

"Thanks for your help," Gunnar replied. "It sounds like you're doing all you can do. By the way, Robert and Bridgett stayed here last night. They seem to have developed a nice relationship in a short time. They're going to the canoe base later today. I'll tell them about the party I want to have sometime in the next few weeks to talk about the canoe trip and update you all on my cancer. Maybe you could mention it to your sisters."

Gunnar was sorting through his fishing gear when Robert and Bridgett stopped by to pick up their suitcases.

"Sorry we can't stay longer but we'll be back," Robert said. "I have to get back to Madison for a meeting on Friday, the 10th, so I'll probably drive straight home on Thursday from Ely after Bridgett leaves. It's an eight- or nine-hour drive to Madison."

"I'm glad you both could visit," Gunnar said. "I'll let you know what we find out about Abigail. I also want to have a get-together with the whole family sometime later this month, to update you on my cancer and to talk more about my canoe trip. We may have some information about Abigail by then, too. I hope so. We'll do it on a weekend at Northland, and you and Bridgett can stay here again."

33

Gunnar kept his appointment with Dr. Lister on August 8 and was happy when the nurse removed the suprapubic catheter. Dr. Lister noted how much better Gunnar looked since his visit a month before. A follow-up appointment was made for August 15, when the new PET scan would be reviewed and a decision for further treatment would be made.

Lucas called on Monday, the 13th, and said he had checked the human resource office at the Lyric mill in Thunder Bay.

"There was no record for William or Bill Fraser having ever worked there, but their files only went back about fifteen years because of a fire years ago that destroyed their older files. The human resource person at the Newton paper mill in Cloquet said a William Fraser had worked *there* thirty years ago, but he died suddenly of a heart attack. I also contacted the volunteer office at St. Benedict's. The lady in charge, Mrs. Lolita Dobbs, recalled there was an Abigail Fraser who worked there as a volunteer, but that was twenty-five years ago. I still have to contact Lake Head University and the canoe factory in Atikokan, and I'm waiting for the results of the fingerprint check of the journal."

"It sounds like the biographical information she told me about herself was all a fabrication," Gunnar sighed. He had to admit he was disappointed. "I'll bet you'll hit a dead end when you check on the other two sources. The Abigail who was **with me on the** canoe trip appeared to me to be about 40 years old. She was attractive and kind, and she lifted my spirits when I was with her. And she saved my life when my canoe ended up at her campsite. When I told her about my cancer, she was supportive and encouraged me not to get depressed or lose faith. I think that's when I started feeling better."

Gunnar had his PET scan on Friday, August 10, and met with Dr. Lister the following week to review the scan.

"The scan does not show any progression of the disease," he said. "You still have evidence of metastases in the lungs and liver, as was noted before. But everything else is the same and the prostate gland is smaller. You need to keep taking the Lupron injections, and I want you to have one more cycle of the Docetaxel. We'll do a repeat scan in six months and I'll see you then. In the meantime, if you have any problems or questions you know to give me a call."

"I do have a question, Dr. Lister," Gunnar said. "Is it a good sign that I am feeling so much better than a month ago?"

"Yes," Dr. Lister agreed. "In one sense, that is a good sign. However, the fact that the cancer has spread to your lungs, liver and lymph nodes is not a good sign. Based on the scan, the cancer has stabilized, at least for the present time. That's good. It means the Lupron and Docetaxel are probably helping. Time will tell. Even though the five-year survival rate for Stage 4 disease may be as high as 40 to 50 percent, the cancer is not curable."

Lucas contacted Gunnar again on August 15.

"I called the HR office at Lake Head University in Thunder Bay yesterday. "Their records show Mrs. Abigail Fraser was on the teaching faculty from 1955 to 1980. She moved to Cloquet with her husband, who got a new job there. Yours were the only set of fingerprints on the journal, Dad. We even checked the watermark on the paper in the journal and traced it to a company from Thunder Bay that went out of business forty years ago. There was also a record of a sale of a solo canoe at the Souris River Factory to Mrs. Fraser, but that was in 1993."

"Thank you, Lucas," Gunnar said. "I can't think of anything further to do, so let's just wait and see what happens. I did get a more or less positive report from Dr. Lister regarding my cancer. It's still present but it hasn't changed since the scan I had before my canoe trip. He wants to see me back in six months unless I start to have a problem."

"That *is* good news, Dad," Lucas said. "And I agree with you; there's not much more we can do now about trying to identify Abigail."

"I would like to go ahead and plan for our family to get together at Northland on Saturday, September 1st, if they have a room available. That's just two weeks from now. I can review my canoe trip and bring everyone up to date on my cancer. Does that sound okay with you? It will be my treat. I also plan to invite Bridgett, and Jack Riley and his wife. Why don't you call your sisters and remind them that spouses and children are also invited. Maybe we'll have some more information about Abigail by then."

CHAPTER

3 4

G unnar picked up Jack and his wife, Carol, at the airport on Friday, August 31. Jack said there were so many cancellations and flight delays because of bad weather that they decided to come to Duluth a day early to make sure they got there for the party. Robert and Bridgett also arrived from Madison on Friday evening. After they got settled, Robert announced to Gunnar that they had gotten engaged.

Gunnar was stunned, though not unpleasantly so. Still, he felt the need to advocate for slowing things down a bit.

"You've only known each other for a few weeks," he said. "Are you sure you're not pushing things too quickly? Your mom and I knew each other for four years before we got engaged."

"I understand what you're saying, Dad, but things are different now," Robert said. "We're both in our thirties and we want to have a family. We talked to Bridgett's folks and they said the same thing, but they understand. We share many things, like you and Mom did. We're both Catholic, we have good jobs, we love the canoe country. Most of all, we love each other very much. It's almost magical how we came to know each other. I asked Bridgett's dad for his blessing and we're asking for yours. We haven't decided when we'll get married, but we both want to be engaged."

"I'm happy for both of you," Gunnar said with a smile. "Of course you have my blessing. I think you'll make an ideal couple.

Why don't you share your good news with everyone tomorrow night at the party."

The party that Saturday night at Northland Country Club was a great success. Before dinner, Gunnar made an announcement.

"After dinner I will tell you all about my amazing canoe trip and update you on the latest report regarding my cancer. When I finish — and I promise I will be brief — Robert has an announcement and our special guest, Congressman Jack Riley, wants to say a few words."

A podium had been set up in the front of the room. As dessert was being served, Gunnar walked up to the podium and addressed the group.

"I want to thank everyone for coming tonight," he began. "I'm thankful for having such a great family. Three weeks is a long time to be alone on a canoe trip. As it turned out, I was alone for only a part of the trip. As the trip progressed, the one thing I missed most of all was you, my family. I came to the conclusion that I am not a fan of solo canoe trips; I like to be with people.

"On the health front, I can report that my cancer is stable. Dr. Lister wants me to stay on medication but he doesn't need to see me again for six months. He was cautiously optimistic about the future. I think the canoe trip was therapeutic, both physically and spiritually. I not only feel better than I have for some time, but I felt connected with Kathleen when I visited some of our favorite lakes and campsites. And I had some great fishing. I caught a northern pike that was so big it pulled me under water and I had to let it go in order to save myself." He waited a beat to judge his audience's reaction. "Now, if you believe that, I'd like to tell you about the black bear that shared my tent with me one night."

That comment got a delayed laugh and Gunnar smiled. He was enjoying himself.

"Seriously, I did catch two trophy northerns, one in Keats Lake and one in Conmee. The walleyes also were plentiful. We caught one beautiful lake trout in Sarah Lake. I actually didn't catch it. It was caught by my friend, Abigail, who I'll mention in a minute.

"I met some wonderful people on the trip, two of whom are with us tonight, Bridgett Olson and Jack Riley. I met Bridgett and Jack on Sturgeon Lake. It was a most amazing coincidence to have met there. As a result of our meeting, I feel we'll be friends for life. The most difficult day of my trip was on Sark Lake, when I almost died from hypothermia. I was rescued by a wonderful lady, Abigail Fraser, who was camped on Sark. Unfortunately, Mrs. Fraser is not here and she seems to have disappeared. She is the one who caught the big laker.

"And that about sums up the trip. Now I'm going to sit down and eat my cheesecake while Robert makes an announcement."

"Thanks, Dad," Robert said after they had traded spots at the podium. "You need to write a book about that canoe trip. I want to talk to you some more about it, too." Robert turned to his audience. "Dad mentioned he met Bridgett Olson on his recent canoe trip. Bridgett was guiding a group of Boy Scouts from Sommers Canoe Base in Ely. Jack Riley and his troop of Scouts were the folks she was guiding. They shared a campsite in Sturgeon Lake with Dad, who asked her to call me when she got back to the canoe base to tell me that Dad was doing okay. It just happened that I live in Madison, where Bridgett also lives and teaches school there. While I had never officially met Bridgett before, I knew her folks, and she and I are neighbors in Madison. I actually talked to her about four years ago when my company was doing some work at her school. Anyway, my announcement is that Bridgett and I have fallen in love and have gotten engaged, all in the space of about three weeks."

There were a few gasps before everyone started clapping. Lucas raised his glass and offered a toast to Robert and Bridgett. Then Gunnar introduced Jack and Carol Riley.

"Jack, please come up here and be recognized," he said. "Jack and his lovely wife, Carol, have made a special trip from Wichita to be with us tonight. As I have already mentioned, Jack and I met for the first time about six weeks ago on Sturgeon Lake in the Quetico, at the same time I met my future daughter-in-law Bridgett. Jack, the stage is all yours."

"Thank you very much, Gunnar," Jack said as he took the podium. "Carol and I are so pleased to be here tonight to meet your family and be a part of this wonderful party. As you all know, Gunnar was an outstanding Marine who served two tours in Vietnam, the first in 1968 and 1969, and the second in 1970. His last deployment was interrupted when he was seriously wounded in an incursion called Operation Imperial Lake. He almost died as a result of those injuries but, through the heroic efforts of Navy corpsmen and the surgeons on the USS Sanctuary hospital ship, he survived. My father, Captain Jack Riley, who was Gunnar's commanding officer at that time, later was killed in the same operation. Before he died, my dad recommended Gunnar for the Congressional Medal of Honor. I would like to read the following:

> *The Medal of Honor is the highest U.S. military*
> *decoration awarded by Congress to a member of*
> *the armed forces for gallantry and bravery in combat*
> *at the risk of life above and beyond the call of duty.*

"For some reason the paperwork that my dad filed got misplaced or put aside in all the confusion as the war was winding down. Gunnar did receive a very prestigious medal, the Silver Star. When Gunnar and I met by chance on the canoe trip, I discovered that Gunnar was the man my dad had recommended for the Medal of Honor — he had mentioned it in a letter he had written to my mom. When I returned to Wichita after the canoe trip I found those letters, which Mom had saved. I contacted the commandant of the

Marine Corps and he consulted the Secretary of Defense. They reviewed Gunnar's service records and determined that there was enough evidence indicating Gunnar was deserving of the Medal of Honor. However, before it can be awarded, it must be approved by Congress and submitted to the president. And, in a case like this where the incident occurred forty-eight years ago, a special act of Congress is necessary. Two weeks ago, I submitted a request to Congress for approval. It passed almost unanimously. Normally, it takes weeks, even months, to get such approval. The rapid response that happened with my request is almost unheard of.

"I am happy and honored, Gunnar Charles Hansen, to announce you will be receiving a call and a letter from President Donald J. Trump, advising that you will be awarded the Congressional Medal of Honor In a special ceremony at the White House very soon."

Gunnar was speechless. This was not what he had expected when Jack said he wanted to say a few words tonight. A tear rolled down his cheek and he reached for his handkerchief to blow his nose. Everyone was standing and clapping. After a few minutes, Gunnar recovered himself. The memory of that day in September 1970 flashed across his mind, along with all the pain and suffering that had happened.

When everyone settled down, Lucas stood up.

"Dad asked me to thank all of you for coming to the party tonight," he said. "For those of you who are able, you are all invited to meet tomorrow afternoon at Dad's house across the street for more details about Abigail Fraser, his mysterious canoeing partner."

35

R obert, Bridgett, Gunnar and the Rileys attended the noon Mass at Holy Rosary Cathedral on Sunday. Jack and Carol had to catch a flight back to Wichita that left at four. They all stopped for coffee and doughnuts after Mass and then dropped the Rileys off at the airport.

"It's been a nice visit, Gunnar; thanks for your hospitality. You have a great family," Jack said as they were about to board. "You should be hearing from Washington this week. One of the liaison folks at The White House told me they were going to send a plane to Duluth to take you and your family and friends to Washington, so don't worry about transportation. Carol and I plan to be at the ceremony. I am so happy we were able to do this for you, Gunnar. It's long overdue."

Gunnar and Lucas spent the rest of the afternoon at Gunnar's house, talking more about his canoe trip and Abigail Fraser and what they had — and hadn't — discovered about her.

Gunnar received a call from President Trump on Wednesday, September 5. He congratulated Gunnar and said they would like to plan the award ceremony the following Friday, September 14. Gunnar thanked him and agreed that would be fine.

Later that day, Pat Bean from The White House liaison office called and said the president had authorized an Air Force plane to pick up Gunnar, his family and guests in Duluth on Thursday, September 13, and fly everyone to Washington.

"You'll be staying at the Willard Hotel while you're in Washington," Ms. Bean said. "I will call you tomorrow to confirm how many will be in your party so we can reserve enough rooms. Thank you for your service, Mr. Hansen. It will be a pleasure to meet you next week. Congratulations."

Gunnar was overcome by emotion and had to sit down for a few minutes to try to absorb everything. Later he called Lucas and asked him to check with everyone who would be going to Washington and give him a list so he could provide the information to Ms. Bean when she called back. He also called Jack Riley to let him know the date and Jack confirmed he and Carol would be there.

September 13 was a beautiful fall day in Duluth. The leaves had changed to various shades of red and gold and the temperature was a comfortable 70 degrees. Gunnar found his old uniform in the back of his closet and was pleased to discover it still fit. During his time in the Judge Advocate General Corps, he had been promoted to the rank of major. He was proud to be a Marine and was looking forward to going to Washington and meeting the president.

The plane landed at Reagan National Airport and the whole entourage was transported in a special bus to the Willard Hotel, just a few blocks from The White House. Besides all of Gunnar's children and their spouses, including Bridgett, the family group included his brother, Antonio; his sisters Anna and Sara; and Kathleen's sisters Elsa and Agnes. Some of the folks from his law firm and the mayor of Duluth and his wife also were in the group, along with Dan and Margaret Hamilton. Jack Riley and his wife flew in from Wichita. A room had been set aside for a private dinner Thursday night at the Willard. Everyone was excited about the ceremony the next day.

The whole group met at noon Friday, September 14, at The White House. Gunnar's guests were escorted to the East Room and Gunnar met the president and first lady in the Oval Office, where the president signed the actual citation. Then they moved into the East Room for the presentation, where he was introduced by President Trump.

"I want to welcome all of you and thank you for being present today on this special occasion, honoring our Medal of Honor recipient, Major Gunnar Charles Hansen, USMC, retired. Major Hansen was born in Austin, Minnesota, on March 7, 1945. He graduated from the University of Minnesota summa cum laude in June 1967 and entered the Marine Corps on September 1, 1967. He was initially deployed to Vietnam from February 1968 until March 1969. He was chosen to attend Officer Candidate School and graduated in August 1969; he was commissioned a second lieutenant. He went on to the Marine Corps Basic School, graduating in February 1970, and was deployed for his second tour of duty in Vietnam in March 1970. He was seriously wounded in combat in September 1970. I would now like to ask General Higgins to come forward to read the citation."

General Higgins, commandant of the Marine Corps, read the citation as a Marine Corps aid held up the actual medal.

"Thank you, Mr. President, for that introduction," General Higgins began. "It is very unusual for me as the Marine Corps commandant to read the citation, but this is a very unusual situation. I asked President Trump if he would allow me to do this honor and he readily agreed. I would like to add some additional information about Major Hansen that some of you in attendance today may not be aware of. The reason we are here today to award the Congressional Medal of Honor is because of a chance meeting between Major Hansen and Congressman Jack Riley on a canoe trip in July 2018 in the Quetico Provincial Park in Canada. Congressman Riley was on a canoe trip with his son and shared a campsite with Major Hansen. At that meeting, Major Hansen talked about his Vietnam experiences. They discovered that Congressman Riley's father was Major Hansen's CO in September 1970, during a major incursion,

Operation Imperial Lake. Major Hansen, then Second Lieutenant Hansen, was seriously wounded that September and Congressman Riley's father was killed that December. Before he died, Captain Riley recommended Second Lieutenant Hansen for the Medal of Honor. Somehow, Captain Riley's paperwork was lost or misplaced, but he did mention his recommendation in a letter to his wife, a letter Congressman Riley remembered his mother telling him about. After determining that Major Hansen was, indeed, the person his father had recommended, Congressman Riley found the letter among the items his mother had saved. He then brought the letter to my attention. Both the Secretary of the Navy and the Secretary of Defense were consulted and, after reviewing Major Hansen's service records, gave their approval to pursue the matter further. Congressman Riley introduced legislation in Congress for approval, which was nearly unanimous. After he recovered from his injuries, Major Hansen stayed in the Marine Corps and attended law school. He distinguished himself in the Marine Judge Advocate General Corps. I will now read the citation:"

> *Major (then Second Lieutenant) Gunnar Charles Hansen, United States Marine Corps, First Platoon, Company E, Second Battalion, First Marine Division, was ordered to engage his Platoon against elements of the North Vietnamese Army and the Viet Cong on 7 September, 1970, during Operation Imperial Lake in Quang Nam Province, Republic of Vietnam. Almost as soon as his Platoon was in position, they began taking heavy machine gun, rocket and mortar fire from the entrenched enemy, especially Squad One. The fighting was described as intense. Second Lieutenant Hansen called for air support and was ordered to pull back by his commanding officer. It became apparent to him that retreating was impossible and air support was delayed. Unable to contact his commanding officer when his radio was destroyed by enemy fire, which also inflicted a severe wound in his right*

*thigh, and without regard for his own safety, he took two car-
tridge belts full of grenades and ammunition and his M-16 rifle
and proceeded on foot along a dry stream bed near where his
men were pinned down and circled around behind the enemy's
position. Lobbing grenades and firing his rifle on full automatic,
he killed or wounded enough of the enemy to allow his platoon to
withdraw to safety just as the air support arrived. Second Lieutenant Hansen continued to engage the enemy until he was shot
in his abdomen and in his left ear and jaw, at which time he lost
consciousness. He was saved from bleeding to death by a Navy
corpsman who managed to stop the bleeding from his thigh and
abdomen until he could be transported to the USS Sanctuary
Hospital Ship, where he underwent emergency surgery. It took
him eight months and numerous operations to recover, except for
a total loss of hearing in his left ear. Second Lieutenant Hansen's
efforts saved many lives and turned the tide of the battle that
day. He demonstrated conspicuous gallantry and intrepidity at
the risk of his own life above and beyond the call of duty, in the
highest traditions of the United States Marine Corps.*

President Trump then placed the Medal of Honor around Gunnar's neck and everyone applauded. Gunnar stepped up to the
podium to thank President Trump and his friends and family for
sharing this moment with him. He said he never felt like he did
anything that day so many years ago to merit such an award.

A grand party was held that night at the Willard, and the entourage returned to Duluth on Saturday, September 15. The Duluth City
Council sponsored an appreciation reception at the Duluth Conven-
tion Center two weeks later and many friends and well-wishers
attended. The Duluth News Tribune ran a series of articles about
Gunnar for a few weeks but, by the middle of October, things had
quieted down. He received a number of inquiries about writing a
book but he turned them all down.

CHAPTER

36

———————

Thanksgiving and Christmas 2018 were happy times for Gunnar, in spite of the unusually heavy snow and subzero temperatures. Robert and Bridgett announced their wedding date to be right after Christmas, on December 29 in Madison. Everyone would be out of school then for the Christmas holiday and they hoped the whole family would be able to attend. The wedding in Madison was a beautiful ceremony with a nuptial Mass. Robert and Bridgett left on their honeymoon on December 30, a week in Florida.

Gunnar was feeling good but noticed he was losing weight again, even though he had a good appetite. He had a repeat PET scan in late January and had an appointment with Dr. Lister on February 14, 2019.

"Gunnar, the scan shows the cancer has not progressed. In fact the lung and liver metastases look like they have decreased in size since August. It appears that Lupron is suppressing the cancer. Let's plan to do a repeat scan in six months and continue with the Lupron."

Gunnar's seventy-fourth birthday was on March 7, 2019, the feast day of his patron saint, St. Thomas Aquinas, the brilliant thirteenth century Italian theologian. One of Gunnar's favorite books, which he read in high school, was *The Dumb Ox*, the biography of St. Thomas, written by G.K. Chesterton. A birthday party for Gunnar was held at Lucas's home on London Road, a beautiful old mansion overlooking Lake Superior. Even Emma was invited. Everyone was excited when Bridgett announced she was pregnant and the baby was due sometime in November. Gunnar was particularly happy about having another grandchild and only wished Kathleen could be there to help him celebrate. Robert and Bridgett took Gunnar and Emma home after the party.

"I had a great time tonight but I'm tired so I think I'll go to bed," he said. "You guys sleep in and I'll make waffles for you when you get up. They're forecasting more snow for tomorrow."

As promised, Gunnar fixed waffles with bacon and real maple syrup and butter for breakfast. He also brewed a pot of Gene Hicks Gourmet Coffee. It started snowing as they sat down to eat.

"How did you sleep, Dad? You look tired," Robert said.

"I'm not sure," Gunnar replied. "I fell asleep as soon as my head hit the pillow, but I kept dreaming about my canoe trip last summer. I kept seeing images of Abigail and talking to her. I woke up once about 3 a.m. to use the restroom. But I went to sleep again as soon as I got back in bed — and the dream started again. Abigail was talking about her journal, but I couldn't understand what she was saying. She was writing in it. Then she gave it to me but I didn't open it. When I finally woke up this morning, I had kicked most of my covers off the bed. It was a restless night."

"Do you remember what you talked about?" Bridgett asked.

"No. Everything seemed so real in my dream but now I can't remember much."

"Have you or Lucas found out anything new about what happened to her since last summer?" Robert asked.

"You might say we've hit a dead end," Gunnar sighed. "I keep thinking about one thing she said to me a number of times. We were talking about how we both liked the mystery stories written by Agatha Christie, Dorothy Sayers and G.K. Chesterton. She said, and I quote, 'You will find the answer to the mystery at the end rather than the beginning.' I didn't think much about it at the time, but I wonder if she was trying to tell me something."

Later that afternoon, Gunnar decided to call Lucas.

"Could you come over sometime," he asked. "I'd like to tell you about a dream I had last night."

Lucas said he had plans with his family Friday evening but he would come by to see Gunnar Saturday morning.

"Please bring the journal with you," Gunnar requested.

Gunnar was just finishing breakfast when Lucas arrived. Robert and Bridgett were upstairs packing, because they had to leave to head back to Madison.

"Thanks for coming by, Lucas," Gunnar greeted him before ushering him into the living room. "The dream I had the other night was about Abigail; it was so real, almost like she was talking to me."

"Since then, I've been thinking a lot about the whole situation with Abigail, particularly in light of something she said to me on the canoe trip. We were talking about our favorite early twentieth-century mystery writers and she commented about finding the answer to the mystery at the end of the story rather than the beginning. When her journal dropped out of my pack sack, I was so surprised, I just gave it a cursory look and called you right away. Have you had a chance to examine it carefully?"

"No, I haven't, Dad," Lucas said. "I turned it over to my friend in the police department to do a fingerprint check. When he finished with it and returned it to me, I put it in my desk drawer and forgot about it."

"I think the journal may be the key to answering the question as to who Abigail is and what happened to her," Gunnar said. "There must be a reason why she left it behind for me to find. Let's look at what she has written."

Lucas handed over the journal and Gunnar opened it.

"It looks like the first half of the journal is a record of her first two canoe trips," he said. "There are two blank pages and then she copied the Wilderness Grace Prayer on the next page. The following page is strange. Look at this."

ABIGAIL'S JOURNAL

July 11, 2018   First Day of canoe trip, Stanton Bay, Pickerel Lake, Quetico

July 20, 2018   Arrived at Sark Lake campsite. I set up camp. Waiting for Gunnar. Am in no hurry.

July 21, 2018   It's dusk. Raining. No sign of Gunnar's canoe. My dog Lizzie is my Guardian. Almost midnight. She is such an Angel.

July 22, 2018   Finally arrived. He's hypothermic. He will survive but is now sick. He Has improved this morning. His Trouble will be resolved.

July 23 2018   Traveling together. Happy. I'll stay with him. Emma and Lizzie Protect us. Good dogs.

July 24, 2018   Joyce Lake. Nice campsite, fresh walleye. Almost like heaven. For now Can enjoy it.

July 25, 2018   Now to Conmee. Dark water; will Stay. Rain again. Wore rain jackets Until rain stops.

July 26, 2018   Fished in Conmee. Big pike. He was excited.

July 27, 2018   Finally got to his McIntyre. He Is
          very happy. Said he feels Safe
          here with Kathleen's spirit.

July 28, 2018   It is a beautiful lake. Clear water. I
          went swimming. Full moon. Will
          miss it. It's something I've Always
          wanted to see from the earth.

July 29, 2108   My canoe was damaged in a storm; will Be
          in Sarah tomorrow. I have enjoyed being With
          him for a few days.

July 30, 2018,   He told me today, "I enjoy being with You."
          Sarah Lake was nice. I caught a trout and we saw a Deer.

July 31, 2018   North Bay and our last campsite. My last words to
          him: "Good night, Gunnar."

"There is a note about starting her trip on Pickerel Lake on July 11th, the same day you started your trip on Beaverhouse, and then no entry until Sark Lake on July 20," Lucas said. "The last entry is on July 31. That would have been your last campsite, when she disappeared. What do you think it means, Dad?"

"I don't know," Gunnar said. "Could it be some kind of code? I keep thinking about her words, 'the answer to the mystery is at the end.' Let's make a copy of this page on the copier in my office."

After they had made a copy, Gunnar and Lucas wrote down the last word on each line of the page, starting with the first entry on July 20. Here's what they found:

I-Am-hurry-Gunnar's-Guardian-Angel-He-Has-Trouble-resolve-I'll-Protect-dogs-walleye-Can-enjoy-Stay-Until-stops-He excited-Is-Safe-spirit-I-Will-Always-earth-Be-With-days-You-Deer-Gunnar-grove.

"Those words lined up together look like some kind of message.

Lucas; see how some words are capitalized," Gunnar said. "Try removing all the words that aren't capitalized. Then underline and highlight the capitalized words that are left and let's see what we have."

July 11, 2018   First Day of canoe trip, Stanton Bay, Pickerel
                Lake, Quetico

July 20, 2018   Arrived at Sark Lake campsite. **I**
                set up camp. Waiting for Gunnar. **Am**
                in no hurry.

July 21, 2018   It's dusk. Raining. No sign of **Gunnar's**
                canoe. My dog Lizzie is my **Guardian**.
                Almost midnight. She is such an **Angel**.

July 22, 2018   Finally arrived. He's hypothermic. **He**
                will survive but is now sick. He **Has**
                improved this morning. His **Trouble**
                will be resolved.

July 23 2018   Traveling together. Happy. **I'll**
                stay with him. Emma and Lizzie **Protect**
                us. Good dogs.

July 24, 2018   Joyce Lake. Nice campsite, fresh walleye.
                Almost like heaven. For now **Can**
                enjoy it.

July 25, 2018   Now to Conmee. Dark water; will **Stay**.
                Rain again. Wore rain jackets **Until**
                rain stops.

July 26, 2018   Fished in Conmee. Big pike. **He**
                was excited.

July 27, 2018   Finally got to his McIntyre. He **Is**
                very happy. Said he feels **Safe**
                here with Kathleen's spirit.

July 28, 2018   It is a beautiful lake. Clear water. **I**
         went swimming. Full moon. **Will**
         miss it. It's something I've **Always**
         wanted to see from the earth.

July 29, 2108   My canoe was damaged in a storm; will **Be**
         in Sarah tomorrow. I have enjoyed being **With**
         him for a few days.

July 30, 2018, He told me today, "I enjoy being with **You**."
         Sarah Lake was nice. I caught a trout and we saw a **Deer**.

July 31, 2018   North Bay and our last campsite. My last words to
         him: "Good night, **Gunnar**."

"It looks like we have something that makes sense," Gunnar said. "Let me read her words — *I Am Gunnar's Guardian Angel* — *He Has Trouble* — *I'll Protect* — *Can Stay Until He Is Safe* — *I Will Always* — *Be With You* — *Deer Gunnar*."

"Wow, Dad." Lucas sounded stunned. "The answer to who Abigail is has been right here in her journal. I guess she figured we would be smart enough to eventually figure it out."

"I'm not sure about that, Lucas," Gunnar said. "If I had not had that dream about her the other night, I don't think I would have thought about looking at her journal again. The interesting thing is there are no entries from July 11th until July 20th. I wonder why."

"Is it possible, Dad, since she is an angel, that she just appeared at the campsite in Sark to meet you there and save you from dying? The whole thing is confusing, especially her story about being a teacher and being married and having children. I guess she had to create some type of deception to hide her true identity. And yet you said she appeared to be as human as you or me."

"I guess anything is possible, Lucas. I know I could not have finished my canoe trip without her help. And, since being with her,

I feel better both physically and emotionally. I'm now sure that the corpsman who saved me all those times in Vietnam was my guardian angel. Remember, Lucas, angels are pure spirits who are neither male or female. So when they appear to us, they may be either a man or a woman. When you think about it, it's reassuring to know they're there. They are messengers sent from God to protect us."

The grandfather clock in the living room started chiming noon as Robert and Bridgett walked into the room. Emma had been sitting on the floor next to Gunnar but barked in greeting as they approached. She ran over to them, seeking attention; they obliged by petting her.

"We're leaving, Dad," Robert said, one hand still on Emma. "We have to get back to Madison. I told you we're looking for a house and we are supposed to meet the Realtor tomorrow."

"Be safe going home," Gunnar said.

"We will," Robert confirmed. "Hey, have you found out anything new from reviewing Abigail's journal?"

"Yes, we have determined that Abigail is my guardian angel who has been protecting me throughout my life," Gunnar said. "It's reassuring to know. In fact, I have always believed that each of us has a guardian angel. What I can't understand is why she appeared to me in human form and accompanied me on my canoe trip. Maybe I'll know someday. It's not important to me now."

"I'm glad you have some answers," Robert said. "We do need to get going though. That was a wonderful birthday party. We've had a great time."

After they left, Lucas said he had to leave, too. He had promised his kids he would take them skiing to Spirit Mountain, a beautiful ski area south of Duluth, that afternoon.

"I'm glad we were finally able to resolve, at least partially, the mystery surrounding Abigail," Lucas said before he left. "I wish I could thank her in person for protecting you."

"I think she knows how you feel," Gunnar said. "Thanks for your help, Lucas."

"Anytime, Dad."

"By the way," Gunnar said before Lucas got completely out the door, "since I've been feeling so much better, I may want to take a canoe trip this summer with some of the grandchildren. Talk to your kids and see if they're interested."

END

Made in the USA
Las Vegas, NV
10 July 2024

92130831R00120